About the Author

Gavin Catt was born in 1970, and lives outside Melbourne, Australia. He is currently employed as a clerical officer at a Melbourne Hospital and he is a qualified dental assistant. Gavin is also a professional songwriter, composer and musician. Gavin enjoys watching and reading science fiction movies and books. His favourite authors are David Brin, Suzanne Collins and Margaret Atwood.

Project Genesis

Gavin Catt

Project Genesis

Olympia Publishers
London

www.olympiapublishers.com
OLYMPIA PAPERBACK EDITION

A CIP catalogue record for this title is
available from the British Library.

ISBN: 978-1-80074-763-0

This is a work of fiction.
Names, characters, places and incidents originate from the writer's
imagination. Any resemblance to actual persons, living or dead, is
purely coincidental.

First Published in 2022

Olympia Publishers
Tallis House
2 Tallis Street
London
EC4Y 0AB

Printed in Great Britain

Dedication

I wish to dedicate this book to my late mother, Patricia, who died in January 2021. Mum read and enjoyed a draft version of my first book 'Sanctuary' before she passed away.

Acknowledgements

Thank you to Aisha Mansfield and Phoebe Bacon for your encouragement. I also would like to thank the dedicated team at Olympia Publishers for your professionalism and encouragement.

Introduction

Three years ago, three important events in my life happened, and each of these events had a profound effect on me. Firstly, I became King of the White Kingdom, which is now known as the White Commonwealth, after my father, King Douglas, was brutally murdered by the Dark Emperor. Secondly, I married my distant cousin, Michelle, who is now known as Queen Michelle Mary 2nd, and the mother of my daughter, Caroline, who is now my heir apparent. Thirdly, my sister, Kathryn, married my cousin, Charles, about one year ago.

Many years ago, Kathryn was engaged to be married to another cousin of mine, Henry, who was my childhood friend, and who had served with me in the Galactic Navy. If I think about it, there is a fourth event, and that is the most important one to me. It was when the Dark Empire and the Dark Emperor was destroyed, and that ended the sixty-year period that the Dark Empire ruled the Milky Way Galaxy with an iron fist.

Quietly, I sit in the audience room of my private office on a normal executive office chair. Two metres away from me is the chair that my visitors sit on. Next to my chair, is a side table with a commlink and a table lamp. The visitor that I am waiting for, could upset the apple cart. Seetar is the Sanctuary Delegate for the mysterious entity, known as 'The Tower'. Normally, I get on very well with Seetar, but the terraforming project of Mars upsets 'The Tower' for some unknown reason. Project Genesis is the only issue that we do not agree on.

Seetar is a Jek human who evolved in the Kiir universe, at the same time as humans did on the Earth. I thought that it was very strange that a Jek, or a human, could be a Sanctuary Delegate for the mysterious sentient machines. Sanctuary could not work this out either. Early on, Seetar had told me that 'The Tower' does not agree with the terraforming project, however he did not say why. I thought that this was strange as 'The Tower' has never objected to any other terraforming project in the universe before.

Contact with any member of 'The Tower' is always through a third party, usually a Sisss, and there is no record of direct contact in Sanctuary Archives. I look at my private assistant. "Has Seetar arrived in the Solar system, otherwise he will be late for this meeting?" I ask.

Checking her screenpad, Assistant Mansfield replies, "He arrived in the Milky Way about one hour ago, and he boarded the shuttlecraft at the Earth System Transfer Station about ten minutes ago. He should be here very soon. The shuttlecraft will be landing on the VIP landing pad here at the White Palace. Seetar has apologised for the delay, as his flight was a commercial IGAL flight from Andromeda."

"Wait a minute. Seetar is a pilot, so is there any information as to why Seetar was on a commercial flight? As a Sanctuary Delegate, he could use his delegation's IGAL starship," I observe, puzzled as to the reason why.

"Queen Noor has removed his flight status, as 'The Tower' has made a formal request," Assistant Mansfield said, with a puzzled look on her face. I nod in answer and before I can reply, my commlink chimes.

"Yes," I answer, not bothering to pick up the handset.

"Sir, Delegate Seetar has arrived at the White Palace and as soon as he clears Security, he will be with you. I will inform you if there is any delay," the Royal Guard Duty Officer says, and then adds quickly, "Your Highness, Delegate Seetar has cleared Security, and he is on his way to you now, escorted by White Palace Security and members of the Royal Guard. Delegate Seetar will be with you in about five minutes."

"Thank you," I reply, as I look at my assistant. Assistant Mansfield nods and turns towards the door, to receive our visitor.

Chapter One:

'Seetar'

"Delegate Seetar has arrived for his audience with you, King William," Assistant Bacon says on the commlink.

"Can you please send him in, Aisha?" I answer.

Assistant Bacon opens the door of the audience room to the outer office; she nods to me, and I nod in reply, and she stands aside to allow Delegate Seetar to enter, accompanied by his escort and his own assistant. Assistant Bacon closes the door behind her, as she leaves the audience room. Assistant Mansfield stands near me, and Seetar stands facing me.

For a moment, I return Seetar's stare, and I gesture to the empty chair facing me, saying, "Please sit down."

"Thank you, King William," Seetar replies, glaring at me. Assistant Mansfield sits down and indicates to me that she is ready to take notes. I look at Seetar expectantly.

"'The Tower' objects to the terraforming project called 'Project Genesis'," Seetar says, with a slightly sharp tone of voice.

Pretending not to notice the tone of voice that Seetar used, I say quietly, "'The Tower' has never objected to any terraforming project anywhere else in the universe before."

"They can object to anything they choose," Seetar says in a patronising way.

I could not understand Seetar's reasons, and it occurs to me that the reason could be personal, as Seetar may not know that Noor told me that 'The Tower' has curtailed some of his privileges as a Delegate.

"'The Tower' has no official presence in this galaxy, nor does it have the right to tell the government of this galaxy what to do!" I say, my voice rising in anger. Seetar smirks.

"Is it because of the Golden Sceptre?" I ask, with annoyance. Seetar sits there quietly, the smirk vanishing from his face, to be replaced by a worried look.

The Golden Sceptre has enormous power, but I did not believe that this is the reason for the objection. Too many things conflicted with what I knew already, and with Seetar's point of view. My own conclusion is that 'The Tower' does not object at all. The other piece of evidence in this mystery is why did Noor remove Seetar's flight credentials? I started to understand that 'The Tower' may want to work with the White Commonwealth. Seetar is the fly in the ointment. Why else would 'The Tower' ask Queen Noor to intervene? 'The Tower' must have some disturbing evidence that Seetar is not what he seems to be.

What I need is a bit of Sherlock Holmes style insight, into the problem. Too bad that Kathryn and Michelle, could not be here. However, Seetar still looks worried. My question is how dangerous is Seetar? Another question comes to mind, can I do anything about it? But I do need to find out if 'The Tower' really objects to Project Genesis, or is it Seetar's own idea, and why is he trying to undermine 'The Tower'?

"The universe could be destroyed," Seetar says, returning my stare. I glance at Assistant Mansfield and the Royal Guards. Their faces convey what I am thinking, 'What is Seetar's point?'. Seetar and I have worked on several Sanctuary Projects together, and I have had some suspicions about him for some time. There is nothing definite that I can think of, as we have agreed on many issues. I decide to test my theory that 'The Tower's' objection is his own idea.

"Seetar, we have worked on many projects together, and I trust you. My question is that, is the objection of Project Genesis your own idea, and not the position of 'The Tower'? Yes, or no?" I ask in a friendly tone. I add quickly, noting Seetar's face darkening in anger, "Without proof that the project will cause a major disaster for the universe, the White Commonwealth will proceed with Project Genesis."

"'The Tower' does not have to explain anything to you, King William. How dare you say that the objection is mine, and not the delegation I represent," Seetar spits out angrily. I return Seetar's glare, but I will not let him provoke me. What he said and how he said it, proved to me that the objection is his own idea, and I still need to get the truth from him. I needed to change my tactics, and defuse the rising tension in the room, and make Seetar answer me without realising that I was suspicious of him.

I shake my head and I yawn. "Seetar, please accept my apology for my rudeness. I could have phrased my question more clearly, and respectfully. Today has been a long and tiring day for me, and my daughter is not well," I say, tiredly. I was exaggerating my feelings slightly. I bow my head slightly, and I sneak a glance at Seetar. The expression on his face changes, and I see a sympathetic look on his face when I sit up straight.

"Please forgive my lack of respect, and I am sure that we can work things out. Sanctuary is aware of the reason why 'The Tower' objects to Project Genesis, and I look forward to seeing you at Sanctuary soon, King William," Seetar says in a considerate voice, and then he adds, "I can try to find out why 'The Tower' objects, and then we can meet to discuss this."

Seetar stands, bows to me, and after nodding to his assistant, he leaves the room.

Once Seetar is out of the room, I remark, "Seetar, I know that you are a bullshit artist, and I know that you are lying." I pick up the commlink handset to call A1 Shentar.

A1 Shentar and I, speak for about half an hour, and I send him a copy of the recording from the meeting with Seetar. A1 Shentar tells me that 'The Tower' had thought that Mars was an ancient relic from the Larip Universe, but their impressions were based on false information that the Karshids had placed in ancient Kiir archives centuries ago. A1 Shentar confirmed that the information in Sanctuary Archives on Mars, is correct. 'The Tower' had informed Sanctuary that they do not object to Project Genesis at all.

"Sa-Sisss has advised me that 'The Tower' wish to apologise to you, and the White Commonwealth. They are requesting a direct meeting with you, King William, and they want to assure you that they have never objected to Project Genesis, and they want to establish diplomatic relations with the White Commonwealth. 'The Tower' is deeply concerned by Seetar's actions and they have advised me that Seetar is wanted for questioning by 'The Tower', and the authorities in the Andromeda Galaxy have also advised me that the Andromedean Security Service will arrest Seetar, on his return," A1 Shentar explains.

"I will contact the Sisss to arrange your meeting with 'The Tower', Will. The meeting will be with 'The Tower' in the Andromeda Galaxy. You'll be right, mate," A1 Shentar says in an Australian accent. We both laugh as we sign off the commcall.

Chapter Two:

'Dinner with Kathryn, Michelle and Charles'

After leaving my office, I walk with my assistants towards the Royal Apartments, and we chat casually. We walk through the courtyard that separates the apartments from the office complex of the White Palace. Normally, I would use the corridors, but I decided that I needed some fresh air. It was late afternoon, pleasantly warm, not too hot and it was sunny. I have always trusted the opinions of my personal staff. Both assistants were returning to their own apartments, and their families. I was aware that both Aisha and Phoebe were looking forward to their own staff minigolf competition. We had been talking about the upcoming tournaments.

We briefly stop at the entrance to the Royal Apartments, and I ask them, "Before you go to your own apartments and other activities, what do you both think of my audience with Seetar?" I could sense that they had been expecting my question, and I note the look that passes between them.

"Put it this way, Your Highness. I would not trust what Seetar told you. There may be a conflict of interest," Assistant Mansfield says.

"Good point, Phoebe," I reply, and I turn to Assistant Bacon.

"I agree with Phoebe, sir," Assistant Bacon says, looking at Assistant Mansfield.

"Thanks, Aisha," I say, nodding to both assistants.

Assistant Bacon adds, "The question is, what is the nature of the conflict of interest? Or is it something more sinister?"

"Bingo," I say in reply.

"I want to thank you both, Phoebe and Aisha. It helps me to gain a different perspective. I would say that I will find out the key to this problem when I have the meeting with 'The Tower'. Enjoy the rest of your day, and have a good evening," I say, smiling. Both women smile in return, and I bid them farewell as I walk towards the door to the Royal Apartments.

'Good night, sir' I hear both assistants say, as I briefly turn to face them, and I say, "Thanks, you guys are the best!" and I turn my attention back to the door, and I enter the Royal Apartments.

I go straight to the Informal Dining Room, realising that Kathryn and Charles would have arrived from Centauri at one p.m., and a clock that I see on the corridor wall showed five p.m. My escort accompanies me to the door, and one member of the escort looks inside the Informal Dining Room. Moments later, after the escort checks the room, the escort guard comes back out and turns to me and nods.

"Did you see my sister or wife in there?" I ask.

"Yes, sir. Your sister and Prince Charles are in the lounge area with Queen Michelle and your daughter," the guard says, noting my smile.

I nod to the guard, and I then enter the Informal Dining Room. As usual, there is momentary silence as I walk through the room, casually greeting people as I go. The silence has always amused me, as I am an ordinary person that just happens to be King and Head of State. Slowly, the noise in the room returns to normal. Once I arrive in the lounge area, I see Kathryn looking in my direction. Michelle sees me as well, and Charles, noticing the looks on Kathryn's and Michelle's faces, turns to face me. "Daddy," cries the shrill pitched voice of my daughter, Caroline, as she runs to greet me. I bend down and I kiss her on her forehead in greeting. The others see this and smile broadly. Caroline takes my hand, and we walk over to Michelle.

I sit down next to my wife, on the sofa that she is sitting on, and I give her a kiss on the cheek. Easing myself forward on the sofa, I give Caroline a hug and I sit back on the sofa. I ask her how school was.

Caroline replies, "It was good, Daddy."

Michelle says to me, "Suzi is coming to take Caroline to have dinner, and if she is good, she will be playing a game of night minigolf too."

"Sounds great," I reply, looking at the eager look on Caroline's face. Caroline was on her best behaviour.

Moments later, Caroline's nanny, Suzi, arrives. She looks at Caroline, and she asks, "Are you ready, Caroline?"

Caroline replies, "Yes, Suzi."

Caroline holds Suzi's hand and Suzi turns to me, saying, "My father has asked me to pass on his good wishes to you, King William."

I look at Suzi and I reply, "That's truly kind of him. Please tell him that I look forward to seeing him when my schedule allows. I will be at the Galactic Navy Minigolf Tournament, and if he is there, I may get the chance to see him. If he is not there, I am sure that I can work something out." Suzi smiles at me and looks down at Caroline's face.

"Ready?" Suzi says to Caroline.

"Yes, Suzi," Caroline answers. Caroline waves at Michelle and I before Suzi leads her away to dinner.

"Suzi's father served under you on board the 'Australis' didn't he?" Michelle asks curiously.

"Her father is Commander Adrian," I reply, as we watch Suzi and Caroline leave the Informal Dining Room.

I knew instinctively that the others were waiting for me to talk about Seetar's audience with me. So, I take the opportunity to kiss Michelle's cheek, causing her to blush.

"Cheeky boy," she says to me.

Kathryn with a smile on her face, asks me, "What happened in the audience with Seetar?"

I frown slightly, and I answer, "It was different. Let us have dinner first before I talk about this. There is to be no shop talk during dinner. I need everyone's input as there is a lot to talk about. After dinner, we can come back here and discuss this."

I stand up, and the others stand also, looking at me, and Michelle says, "Yes, Your Highness." The others nod and we take our seats in the dining area.

During dinner, we make small talk and every now and then Michelle glances at me, raising her eyebrows, which showed her curiosity. I cock my head in the direction of the lounge area, and I nod silently.

Chapter Three:

'The Plan'

After dinner, Kathryn, Charles, Michelle and I return to the lounge area. I noted that there were not many people in the lounge area tonight. None of the 'C' shaped arrangements of three sofas were occupied. However, several tables had a couple of people. 'It's still early,' I think as I sit down. I noted the look of anticipation, that I could see on the faces of my wife and sister, as well as Charles.

I discuss in precise detail, every aspect of my audience with Seetar, and I add the crucial information from my commcall with A1 Shentar. After speaking for about twenty minutes, I ask the others, "What do you think?" For a few moments, there was silence. I watch my wife, sister and Charles look at each other, but I could see that someone was about to speak.

Kathryn says, with a thoughtful look on her face, "It's an interesting situation, Will." Problem was, I was looking at Michelle at the time, so I refocus my attention, on my sister.

"You are quite right," I say, and then I ask, "What about A1 Shentar's suggestion that I go and meet with 'The Tower', because they want to establish diplomatic relations with the White Commonwealth?"

"Cousin William, it sounds to me that you are worried about being in direct contact with 'The Tower' collective, despite the fact the Sisss will be facilitating the meeting," Charles says.

"I am concerned about the safety of this galaxy, and all beings that call the Milky Way Galaxy home," I reply, pausing for a moment, and then I add, "I do not completely trust 'The Tower', but as A1 Shentar is not worried, I have decided that I will go to this meeting."

"What seems strange to me, Will, is why did Queen Noor removed Seetar's flight credentials?" Michelle asks, putting a hand on my shoulder as she spoke.

I lightly touch Michelle's knee, saying, "You're right. I am expecting an answer from Noor at any time."

As soon as I spoke, my screenpad beeped, and then I read the message that had just arrived. I look at the others, and I explain, "The message is from Noor. The reason why Seetar is now wanted by the Security Service in Andromeda, is that he has embezzled millions of credits from his delegation. 'The Tower' has washed their hands of him, and as his commercial flight is thirty minutes away, Noor's authorities will detain Seetar when he arrives."

I look at the stunned looks on Michelle's, Kathryn's and Charles's faces.

"I have not told you the best bit," I say, seeing the looks of confusion.

"Which is?" Michelle asks.

"The Karshids are looking for him too. Seetar was a low-level drug dealer, who thought that he could make some money on the side, by siphoning off a small piece from every sale he made, which upset the clan. Seetar thought that Sanctuary did not know about his criminal activities," I explain.

"How did Sanctuary find out?" Kathryn asks.

"The Shadow told Sanctuary, about three years ago," I answer, with a smirk.

Kathryn notes the look on my face, which makes her grin.

"It was you, wasn't it?" Kathryn asks.

I look at Kathryn, and I reply, "I knew all along that Seetar was a crook, and a traitor to his delegation and to Sanctuary. It was A1 and C3 Shentar's idea, that I watch Seetar closely, to gain his trust and to report to the Permanent Council of Sanctuary."

"So Seetar never suspected anything?" asks Michelle.

"Nothing at all," I answer, looking at my wife.

"What an idiot. Did he have any connection to the Dark Emperor?" Charles asks.

I exchange a glance with Michelle, and then I reply, "He was on Drago's personal staff, at the Maldar Citadel." I see the surprised looks on Kathryn's and Charles's faces. I exchange a knowing look with Michelle.

"Seetar was behind the assassination attempt on me, three years ago on Shentar Two," I say, carefully.

Kathryn gives me a puzzled look.

"How do you know that?" Michelle asks, exchanging a look with Kathryn.

"The Sanctuary Security Service was tipped off about six months ago, by a former associate of Seetar. That is all that I can say on the subject, because the informant was in Galactic Navy Intelligence, who died mysteriously in an air transporter accident recently," I say, looking at the floor in front of me.

Kathryn, Charles, Michelle and I sit in silence for a couple of minutes. I order a drink from a servbot, and I noticed a change in the others as they were looking at me closely, and I could tell that they were concerned that they had upset me. I knew that Michelle knew the circumstances about the death, and that I did not like to talk about it as Michelle and I knew the informant personally. My drink arrives from the bar, and after the servbot moves away, Kathryn changed the subject.

"When is your meeting with 'The Tower' scheduled, Will?" Kathryn asks.

"Within the next few days. A1 Shentar will let me know soon," I say, looking at my sister. For a moment, I think very carefully, and then I ask, "When I do hear from A1 Shentar, why don't you and Charles, come with me to Andromeda? You could spend a few days with Noor, while I go to my meeting, and then after the meeting, I will return to Freedom Hall, and we can head home the next day. Michelle will need to stay here, and I have promised her that we will go somewhere together soon. Besides, I do not think that it is a particularly good idea, bringing Caroline on such an occasion." Michelle gives me a funny look, knowing that I would want her with me, but as this mission could be dangerous, Michelle understood that I would not want to put Caroline in danger.

I look at Charles and Kathryn, as Kathryn and Charles exchange a look. Kathryn smiles and says to me, "We would be happy to go. Someone has to make sure that you behave yourself." Kathryn laughs, seeing the expression on my face.

I put my arm around Michelle's shoulder, and I say to her, "Next time, I promise that you can come," and I kiss Michelle on the cheek.

"All right, cheeky boy," Michelle says in a mock serious tone, and then she kisses me on the cheek in reply.

I say, "Don't forget that the flight skills testing is coming up while you are here," looking at Kathryn and Charles, and then I continue, "The official launch of Project Genesis is a few days after the flight skills testing. Lastly, how can I forget the fly-off challenge, and the minigolf."

Kathryn and Charles look at each other, and then Kathryn

says to me, "Don't feel pressured. Remember to relax. Charles and I will be your backup on this historic occasion." I gratefully nod my head in thanks, and I see the look on Michelle's face, knowing that I would want her to be with me on this flight, and she nods her head in encouragement, while touching my arm, with her hand.

It was right at this moment when I spotted Rebecca and Elizabeth talking on the 'C' shaped arrangement of sofas next to ours. I stand up, while holding a finger up, to indicate 'could you please give me a moment' and I walk over to Rebecca and Elizabeth, and I ask them to join us. They both nod and they stand and follow me back to the others, who were waiting patiently. Rebecca and Elizabeth greet the others, and they sit down. We bring them up to date on the discussion. Rebecca and Elizabeth offer to keep Michelle company, while the rest of us are in Andromeda.

Later, in our apartment, after refreshing ourselves for bed, we lie down on the bed, facing each other.

"Next adventure you have, we are all going," Michelle says, pointing at my chest.

"Yes, boss!" I say, in a mock serious tone of voice. Michelle gives me a sceptical look, and then she grins at me when I say, "I will make it up to you, my love."

"How about right now?" Michelle asks mischievously.

"Okay," I say before I kiss Michelle.

Chapter Four:

'Planning for Departure'

The next day, I advise the Council of Crowns about the upcoming meeting with 'The Tower' in Andromeda, and they pledge their full support, already aware of the necessity of the mission and its benefits. They knew that I understood the risks.

After breakfast the next morning, Kathryn, Charles and I start planning the flight, even though I was unsure as to when the meeting with 'The Tower' would occur. We were in the sitting room of my private apartment, and we were assisted by Rebecca and Elizabeth, and Michelle was there too, but for a different reason. Michelle knew that I was planning a joke on my sister, and every now and then, Michelle exchanged a look with me. Michelle knew that I was planning to use a certain IGAL starship that I have used before.

Rebecca asks me, "Which ship are you planning to use, Cousin William?"

I glance at Michelle, and then I look at Rebecca and I answer, "The 'Raptor'," watching Kathryn's face.

No reaction at all, so I look at Michelle and I see Michelle looking at Kathryn, and I realised that the joke was on me.

There was total silence, the others watching intently. I laugh nervously to break the tension, and to the credit of everyone in the room, nothing needed to be said. Facing Michelle, I wondered why my joke backfired, and I realised that Kathryn and Michelle knew my sense of humour, only too well.

Charles asks me, "'Raptor' is the ship that you used on the Virex and Gemini mission, isn't it?" Silently, I was grateful that Charles asked this question.

"That's correct, Charles," I answer, seeing the look on Kathryn's face. Her eyebrows were raised, and then she smiled at me. I nod, knowing that Kathryn knew what I was thinking. I look at the others and I say, "Thank you for your input. We have covered as much as we can, without knowing the date and time of the meeting. Based on A1 Shentar's information, we will get around forty-eight hours advance notice, so Kathryn and Charles, you will need to be prepared to depart within the next three days."

Kathryn and Charles look at each other, and then they look at me, and Kathryn says, "Yes, Your Majesty. After lunch, Charles and I are going for a couple of rounds of minigolf. If anyone wants to join us, feel free to do so." I look at Michelle, and she nods.

"We will join you," I say to my sister.

After the minigolf game, I had a long audience with Cirek, who is the daughter of King Gyros, the leader on board the 'Wanderer'. The audience finished late, and I saw that the time on the audience room clock was just after six p.m., and I was angry and tired. I wanted to relax and have my evening meal. The family would have started dinner by now, and I did not want to be a killjoy, but I also needed contact with my wife and family.

Slowly, I make my way to the Informal Dining Room, and I go straight to a vacant table, and I sit down. For a few minutes, I just sit there, trying to decide what I will have for dinner. Out of the corner of my eye, I see Kathryn, Michelle and Rebecca coming over to me from a nearby table. As I entered the room, I had already seen Queen Noor's younger sister, Susan, sitting at

Kathryn's table talking to Charles. Susan stayed with Charles, but she watches my wife and sister going over to my table.

They could see that I was in a bad mood, and I noted the looks of concern on their faces. Kathryn asks gently, "Are you okay, Will?" I just shrug my shoulders. Kathryn suggests that I come over and join the others. I say nothing, and I look at the faces of Kathryn, Michelle, Charles, Susan and Rebecca closely, and I could see that they were quite worried about me.

"Have you eaten, Will?" Michelle asks kindly, looking into my eyes.

"No, my love," I say quietly, shaking my head.

Rebecca says, placing a hand on my shoulder, "I will get something for you. Please come over and join us, you need to eat."

I nod my thanks, and I stand and follow Kathryn and Michelle to their table, and I sit down. Rebecca was on her way back with an Informal Dining Room Attendant, carrying a tray with the evening meal on it. The staff are never told who the meal is for, which ensures my safety. The young attendant places the tray in front of me nervously. Something switches in my mind, and I ask, "You're new?" trying to be friendly, considering the bad mood that I was still in, but thankfully, I was already feeling much better.

"Yes, Your Majesty. I started working here a few weeks ago after being transferred from Centauri, after the merger of the two White Palaces there. I chose to come here," the attendant replies to me, still unsure what to say.

I knew from personal experience what it is like to be the odd one out, so I say, "Please don't be nervous. I am sure that you do your job very well. Just relax and be yourself. Take every opportunity to learn new things, and if you do that, everything will work out for you."

In a strange twist, I found encouraging the attendant, helped me to feel much better. The attendant smiles, saying, "Thank you, sir," and then she moves away, attending to her duties. The others sit down, smiling at the transformation, and they watch me eat.

Once I finish eating, a servbot takes my meal tray away and I sit back, feeling much better. I tell Kathryn, Michelle, Charles, Susan and Rebecca, what had happened during my audience with Cirek. "You looked incredibly angry, Will. I can see why you were angry, under those circumstances," Michelle says, and the others nod in agreement.

"You were very nice to the new attendant too," Kathryn adds with a smile. I nod, unsure where the conversation is going, but I knew that this is a sign of tiredness in me.

Kathryn orders a coffee from a servbot, and looking in Charles's direction, I say, "I see that Charles is talking to Susan," as I watch Susan and Charles have their own conversation.

"That's right. He told me that Susan plans to visit Centauri, on her way back to Andromeda. Susan's cousin is there now, and he wants to catch up with Susan, before he returns home to the Vega Galaxy," Kathryn replies. I know that the Vega Galaxy is so remote from Sanctuary, and the Milky Way Galaxy, that it takes six weeks to get there at high IGAL speed, and one Earth year at low IGAL speed, and that is from Sanctuary, not the Milky Way. The only way to get there quickly, is by Trans Dimension or Trans Universe Drive, and if you use that method, it only takes one hour, and no time dilation.

Michelle asks me, "You have been to Vega twice, if I remember correctly?"

"That's right. In both cases, they were both before you joined me at Sanctuary. The sightseeing there is breathtakingly beautiful, and the beings are friendly. Sanctuary has several starships that have the capability to make the trip. 'Swordfish' has been out there a couple of times since we came back from our honeymoon trip." Michelle shakes her head sadly, and Kathryn and Rebecca laugh. Michelle and I exchange a look, and neither of us could keep a straight face, and we started laughing too.

It was at this moment that my personal commlink chimes. "Yes. What is it?" I ask.

"Sorry to disturb you, sir. A1 Shentar has called, he has advised me that your meeting with 'The Tower' is in seventy-two hours from now. Sanctuary has advised Queen Noor that you are coming, as 'The Tower' closest to the Milky Way is on Brioche, in the Andromeda Galaxy," says the voice of Assistant Bacon.

"Thanks, Aisha," I reply, and I sign off. I look at the expectant faces of my wife, sister and cousins, and I say, "We have to leave here in forty-eight hours from now. After breakfast tomorrow morning, we need to finalise our plans and we will leave twenty-four hours later, at eight a.m."

After breakfast the next morning, I contact the Chief Engineer in the White Palace Military Hangar to prepare 'Raptor' for departure in forty-eight hours, and I catch up with Kathryn, Michelle, Charles and Rebecca. We go over the plans for the flight to Brioche, and we find that we only had to update a couple of points. It was now lunch time, and we had the rest of the day to relax or catch up with appointments.

During family time that afternoon with Michelle and Caroline, Caroline says quite forcefully, "I want to come with you, Daddy."

"Caroline, I need you to stay here to keep your mother company; your aunts, Kathryn and Rebecca, will help you. When you are older, you can come," I say, watching the neutral expression on Michelle's face.

"When you are older, you will be doing things that I could never do," I say gently, seeing the look on Caroline's face soften. She kisses me on the cheek, and her nanny arrives to take Caroline to dinner. I embrace Michelle, and we kiss lightly, and I suggest, "Let us go and have dinner. The mission briefing is at eight p.m., and later you and I can have some personal time," I say in a mysterious way.

"We shall see," Michelle says, laughing.

Chapter Five:

'Departing for Andromeda'

After a restful night, I was woken by my alarm at six a.m. Quietly I get up, trying not to wake Michelle and I refresh myself. Dressed casually, I go to the Informal Dining Room for a quiet breakfast. After selecting what I want from the autochef, I sit down at a nearby table. As I eat, I check the news net sites on my screenpad, and after finding nothing that attracted my attention, I finish my breakfast and I talk casually to members of my personal security.

It is at this moment a very tired looking Rebecca enters the Informal Dining Room. She brightens when she sees me, and she comes over to my table.

"You look exhausted, Becky," I say, with concern. She nods and she goes over to the autochef, and gets a coffee, and brings it over to my table. She stands in front of me, and I nod to indicate that she could sit down. She takes a cautious sip of her coffee, and she puts it on the table.

"Busy night?" I ask.

"Fourteen hours straight in the Emergency Department, and I am glad to be heading back to my apartment; I have already let Michelle know that I will be with her after lunch, and after catching up on some sleep," Rebecca says while yawning. We chat casually for a few minutes, and I check the time on the nearby wall clock: 7.10 a.m.

"Thanks again for offering to help Michelle with Caroline. I appreciate it," I say, smiling.

Rebecca smiles, and says, "You are welcome, Your Majesty."

I nod and I say, "I had better go back to my apartment, as I need to leave the apartment by seven forty-five a.m. Kathryn and Charles are joining me in the White Palace Military Hangar at eight fifteen a.m. I would love to stay and chat to my favourite cousin, but I do need to get going."

Rebecca noted the sound of disappointment in my voice, and she says, "I will be fine. You have the hardest job on your plate meeting with 'The Tower' and I know that you will be fine, Cousin Will." I stand smiling, and Rebecca stands, and she shakes my hand, and I kiss her on the cheek and then I leave the Informal Dining Room.

I go back to my apartment, and I enter the bedroom. Michelle is awake and sitting on the edge of the bed, yawning.

"Good morning, my beautiful Queen," I say in a bright and cheery voice. Michelle gives me a fixed stare, and then she starts to smile.

"Sorry if I woke you earlier, my love," I say, thinking that I may have woken her.

She says, trying to stifle a yawn, "You needn't worry about that. I was already awake. Just wondering how your meeting will go. I know that you would want me there, under normal conditions, but I understand the potential dangers involved."

I sit down next to her, saying, "Thanks for that. Rebecca told me that she spoke to you."

"That's right, sweetheart," Michelle says, and then she adds, "Everything will be fine. I will be fine, Caroline is having breakfast with me, in about ten minutes."

"I was going to ask you about that," I say, looking at the clock: seven forty-five a.m. on the wall clock.

"I have to go now; you take it easy and relax. Rebecca and Susan are here to help you if you need it. Ann and Elizabeth have offered to help you too," I say, in an apologetic tone and I put my arm around my wife, and I kiss her on the cheek. We both stand and we kiss passionately.

"Please come next time, my love," I plead in a funny voice. Michelle gives me a fixed stare again and yawns, and I can tell that Michelle is still half asleep.

"What's on your schedule?" I ask. Michelle's expression changes as she thinks.

"I have a nine a.m. meeting and then Caroline and I are playing minigolf before lunch," she says, looking at me.

"Say hi to Noor for me," Michelle says, looking at me.

"I will, my love. Seriously, I wish you could come with me, as your input is always valuable," I reply as I put my hand on her shoulder.

"You will be fine, Will. Take it easy and I will see you in a few days," Michelle says considerately.

"Okay, boss!" I reply. Michelle laughs, gives me a kiss, and I turn to leave, heading for the door to the Royal Apartments corridor.

On arrival in the White Palace Military Hangar, I ask the Chief Engineer if the 'Raptor' is ready for flight.

"Yes, sir. Everything is ready for flight," she replies.

"Have you seen my sister or Prince Charles yet?" I ask, looking at a digital clock on a nearby wall, indicating eight fifteen a.m.

"Not yet, Your Highness," answers the Chief Engineer. I see my sister and husband, enter the hangar.

"There they are," I say. The Chief Engineer nods, and then resumes her duties as Kathryn and Charles stand in front of me.

"Good morning, sleepyheads," I say, good naturedly. Kathryn stares at me and Charles laughs. Charles's laughter is silenced by a glare from Kathryn and then Kathryn and I stare at each other intently. I make a funny face, which makes Kathryn burst out laughing. Looking at Charles, I say to Kathryn, "It's time to go." Kathryn nods, and we walk towards the 'Raptor' at its parking stand.

'Raptor' looks like a NASA Space Shuttle from the late twentieth century, combined with the looks of a F117 Stealth fighter. It is the same size as a Boeing 787 Dreamliner. Kathryn has seen the 'Raptor' before, and she watches Charles stare, opened mouthed at the IGAL starship. Using the boarding ramp, we enter the ship, and we go straight to the flight deck.

"Prepare for departure," I announce.

Kathryn and Charles look around the flight deck, with stunned looks on their faces. Kathryn turns to me, saying, "It is no wonder why you have been so coy about the 'Raptor'."

Grinning, I say, "Now you know how I was able to get so close to the 'Guardian' on the Virex and Gemini mission. The flight deck is smaller than one on a darkship or a lightship. Blueships and Clearships operate with a crew of five, or one crew member can operate the entire ship. Repairs and Maintenance is by engineerbots and maintainabots," I say excitedly.

"You are sounding like a car salesperson again, Will," Kathryn says, grinning.

I stand by the Command Chair in the front row. The other station in the front row is for the co-pilot. The row behind has the Engineering, Science and Weapons stations.

"Kathryn, you are the co-pilot on the way out, and Charles,

you have the Science and Engineering stations, so I suggest sitting at the Science station, and remote the Engineering station to the Science Station. 'Raptor' can be operated by just one person, as I have mentioned," I state, pointing at the stations. Kathryn and Charles nod, and sit at their respective control pads.

I sit down in the Command Chair, and I activate my control pad.

"'Raptor' prepare for departure," I order.

"Ready for departure," the ship replies.

"Auto coms for departure," I request.

"Coms auto for departure," the 'Raptor' answers.

Looking at Kathryn and Charles, I ask, "Are you both ready for departure?"

"Yes, sir," they reply. I touch the external coms icon on my control pad.

"'Raptor' is about to depart," booms my voice in the hangar and I watch hangar staff clear the area surrounding the ship.

"'Raptor' is cleared to depart the hangar," the Hangar Controller says.

With ease and precision, I raise the 'Raptor' off the hangar floor, and I ease the ship forward slowly. Once clear of the hangar, I retract the landing skids, and I pull back on the control column slightly. The altitude increases to five thousand feet, and then I level off, so that once we are twenty kilometres away from the White Palace, I pull back the control column further to a fifty-degree angle, and by activating the sublight systems by voice, we increase our speed as the 'Raptor' climbs up through and leaves the Earth's atmosphere.

Turning to Kathryn, I say, "Kathryn, you have control. Take us out of the solar system. Don't scratch the paintwork!" Kathryn smiles at the ongoing joke between us, and Charles has a confused look on his face.

Kathryn replies, "I have control, and no scratches on the paintwork," and then Kathryn and I laugh, compounding Charles's confusion.

"'Raptor', Auto Control once clear of the solar system, and for IGAL flight to Andromeda," Kathryn adds, looking at me for confirmation.

"Control request acknowledged. Transit time to Andromeda at low IGAL speed, is two hours," the 'Raptor' replies.

I am pleased with the way Kathryn handles the unfamiliar systems.

"You are doing fine, Kathryn," I say to encourage my sister.

"Thanks, Will. You're a great teacher," Kathryn says with a smile.

"We have cleared the solar system. Auto Control is engaged," the 'Raptor' announces. We now have two hours to relax before we are on approach to the Andromeda Galaxy.

Chapter Six:

'Approach and Arrival at Andromeda'

At the halfway point of our journey to the Andromeda Galaxy, Kathryn, Charles and I sit in the crew lounge, relaxing and enjoying a coffee. I was enjoying an English Breakfast tea, and we were casually chatting. Charles makes a remark that under normal circumstances, I would have laughed off. However, on this occasion, my mind is focused on the meeting that I am about to have with 'The Tower'. Kathryn and Charles were going to spend some time with Queen Noor at Freedom Hall. I was looking forward to seeing my close friend too, but my mind is distracted. 'The Tower' completely occupied my thoughts.

Charles leaves the crew lounge to refresh himself, so I take the opportunity to discuss my concerns with Kathryn. Kathryn knew that I hated making speeches, and she sympathised. She also knew that I accepted the fact that I did need to do them. Kathryn understood that when I focus on a task, I tend to close off my mind to anything else.

When Charles returns, I stand without making a comment, and I leave the crew lounge. I return to the flight deck, and I sit down at my control pads, sitting in silence and enjoying the solitude.

I had been sitting, looking out the viewport, at Andromeda, only one hour away at our current speed for nearly fifteen minutes. Checking the different systems on the viewscreens in front of me, at the back of the control pads, I find nothing unusual. Kathryn and Charles enter the flight deck, fifteen minutes after I returned.

"Here he is," I hear Kathryn say, as I was still looking out the viewport.

"King William, I would like to apologise for the remark that I made, it was out of order," I hear Charles say.

Slowly, I turn around in my Command Chair, and looking straight at Charles, I say quietly, in a flat tone of voice, "I need everyone on board this ship, not to lose sight of the task ahead. No exceptions." I stare at Charles, saying nothing further. I start to turn around to face my viewscreens again, when I see Kathryn and Charles exchange a look.

Pretending that I did not see the exchange between Kathryn and Charles, I complete turning my Command Chair around to face the viewport.

"King William, I am sorry that I have upset you. Please accept my apology, it will not happen again," Charles says, in an apologetic tone.

"It had better not, Prince Charles," I say, with disgust.

One hour later, a double tone sounds, and the 'Raptor' announces, "We are now on approach to the Andromeda Galaxy."

"Continue on current course, on auto control and auto coms. Once we are in the Freedom Solar System, switch to manual control for landing," I request.

"Acknowledged, sir," the ship replies.

Just outside the Freedom Solar System, the 'Raptor' is greeted by fighters from the Andromeda Security Service. I thank the Sanctuary Security Service escort for their assistance as they guided me to the Freedom System, and the 'Raptor' enters the Freedom Solar System alone, as I take control for our arrival. The

'Raptor' crosses the orbits of three of the seven planets in the solar system, and we enter orbit of the Freedom planet itself.

To Kathryn and Charles, I say, "Prepare for arrival," and then we start to descend into Freedom's atmosphere. Five minutes later, we land at Freedom Hall itself. I send a quick voice message to Michelle, "Michelle, we have arrived, my love. I will be home in a couple of days, Will."

Chapter Seven:

'Noor'

Kathryn, Charles and I exit the 'Raptor' via the boarding ramp. Standing a few metres away from the end of the boarding ramp, Queen Noor watches Kathryn, Charles and I walk down the ramp, and we step off the ramp together.

"That's one small step for man, one giant leap for mankind," I say quietly, quoting Apollo 11 Astronaut, Neil Armstrong. Kathryn turns her head to face me and just rolls her eyes, in mock disapproval, as we continue to walk over to Noor. I stand two metres away from Noor, facing her. I notice Kathryn and Charles standing next to me, waiting for me to speak.

"Welcome to the Andromeda Galaxy, King William 4th, Head of State of the Milky Way Galaxy," Noor says, smiling broadly, and then she looks at Kathryn and says, "Welcome Queen Kathryn 1st and Crown Prince Charles of Centauri."

"Thank you, Queen Noor, Head of State of the Andromeda Galaxy," I reply, returning Noor's greeting, when Noor faces me again. Noor shakes Kathryn's and Charles's hands. The four of us stand together, facing a waiting band that plays the White Commonwealth Anthem, and then they play the Anthem of Andromeda.

The boarding ramp of a nearby surface transporter, extends out from the vehicle and lowers, allowing us to board the surface transporter. Once we are inside the transporter, the door we entered through closes and we sit down, and we start chatting.

Noor is three years younger than I am, and we were remarkably close when we were younger. We grew up together, when her father was Ambassador to the Milky Way, at the time. In our teenage years, we dated for a while and then we lived together. When it came time for her to return home to Andromeda, we started to drift apart. Knowing that a long-distance relationship was difficult, we remained exceptionally good friends, and both families knew all along about our relationship in the past.

As Noor and I chatted, I remembered our past, and I know Noor did too. Noor is human, with dark brown hair, permed and secured in a bun by a claw clip. Looking at Noor, and if you did not know that she was not born on Earth, you could safely assume that she was born in either Mauritius or French Polynesia, or possibly India, when you look at her. Noor is wearing a light blue three-quarter sleeve business blouse, and a black knee length leather skirt, and black leather knee high boots. Looking at her, if you did not know that she was the Head of State, you may think that Noor was going out with friends. Noor's husband is my cousin, King Edward.

During the time that Noor and her father lived on Earth, her mother, Queen Tarah, stayed at Freedom Hall, attending to royal duties on behalf of her husband. Frequently, Noor's mother and father swapped responsibilities while Noor stayed at the White Palace. Michelle and Kathryn both know about our previous relationship, as Noor and I had told them, and they both knew that I would have married Noor if she had stayed on Earth.

The weather for our arrival on Freedom, was fine and sunny, and twenty-one degrees centigrade.

As the surface transporter moves silently towards the

Freedom Hall Complex, Noor leans closer to me, and asks me, "Are you all set to meet with 'The Tower'?" Charles and Kathryn sit in silence, watching Noor closely.

"Yes. A1 Shentar has told me that a Sanctuary Security starship, will accompany me to Brioche," I reply, noting that Charles was staring at Noor strangely.

Noor answers, pretending not to notice Charles staring at her. "Good, I wish you well, Will. My Tower advisor will answer any questions that you have," Queen Noor says, as the surface transporter arrives at the VIP Entrance to Freedom Hall.

After Queen Noor, Kathryn, Charles and I have a quiet evening meal together; we adjourn to the VIP Lounge for a quick drink. From the time we arrived at Freedom Hall, I had been meeting with Noor's Tower advisor for several hours and I had some quiet time in my quarters, before dinner. During the meal, I had noticed Charles behaving in a strange way, which appeared to make Noor uncomfortable. Kathryn had noticed it too, so it was no surprise when Kathryn asked me if she could have a private word with Charles. I give my consent, and Noor nods in agreement.

Noor and I watch Kathryn and Charles have an intense conversation.

Turning to Noor, I say, "Noor, I have to apologise for my idiot brother-in-law. I could tell that he had been making you feel uncomfortable. On the way here, I had to speak to him about his conduct."

Noor replies, "He was leering at me when Kathryn was not looking. Your brother-in-law is a sleaze. Watching Kathryn give him a serve, hopefully teaches him a lesson."

After about five minutes, Kathryn and Charles return. Charles stands before Noor, and looking at the floor, Charles says, "Queen Noor, I have caused you distress, and I want to apologise for my behaviour." I did not even have to look at Noor, to know that she still felt uncomfortable.

Looking up at Charles, I snarl, "Charles, you have caused distress again on this trip. I do not have the time, to have to speak to you again and again, about your behaviour. If you ever do this again, you will have to answer to the Council of Crowns. Until I return from Brioche, Prince Charles, you are suspended from all royal duties, and you are confined to your quarters, now get out of my sight!"

The look of horror on Charles's face, was satisfying as he turned around to face Kathryn.

"Charles, I may decide to send you home, if I have problems with you again," I say, as Charles nods slowly, looking sheepishly at me.

Kathryn steps forward, and apologises for her husband, and as she turns to go with Charles back to their quarters, Kathryn gives me an apologetic look. After Kathryn and Charles leave the VIP Lounge, Noor thanks me, and to change the subject, we chat casually. The release of tension in Noor's face was evident, and she appeared to be happy again. I could tell that she was pleased that justice was done, regarding Charles.

Kathryn returned to the VIP Lounge ten minutes later, and she sits down opposite me.

"I'm sorry about this, Will. I do not know what has gotten into Charles lately. Please accept my apology, on Charles's behalf. He has agreed to make a formal apology tomorrow, to Queen Noor and to you, Will," Kathryn says, with a sigh.

Noor says, "Kathryn, you have nothing to apologise for," and Noor turns to me, saying, "Will, I think Charles has learnt his lesson."

Looking at Kathryn, I say to Noor, "I plan to rescind the suspension when I return from my meeting with 'The Tower' on Brioche. Kathryn, he needs to remain confined to quarters until I return."

Kathryn nods, knowing that I was being fair to Charles, and that I want him to remember that he needs to behave appropriately, and she replies, "Yes, sir."

Chapter Eight:

'Encountering "The Tower"'

The sun had already risen when I woke up at six thirty a.m. at Freedom Hall. Quietly, I have breakfast alone in the VIP Lounge, and I saw no sign of my sister, or Charles. 'Raptor' had already been checked out overnight for my flight to Brioche, by White Palace and Sanctuary technicians. These technicians had also checked out the Sanctuary IGAL starship that is escorting me to Brioche.

After breakfast, I returned to my apartment to refresh myself and dress casually for the flight. I board a waiting surface transporter that takes me from the VIP Apartments entrance to the Freedom Hall Spaceport. The transporter stops near the 'Raptor', and I disembark. Looking around, I can see that it is still quiet, and I see that the VIP Passenger Terminal is also quiet, and I stand waiting for the boarding ramp to lower, as I have already confirmed my identity to the 'Raptor'. Once the boarding ramp has lowered, I start to walk up the ramp and into the ship, and the boarding ramp retracts as I go straight to the flight deck.

As I sit down at the Command Pilot's Station, I say, "Good morning, 'Raptor'. Initiate pre-flight sequence. Auto Start and Manual Control for take-off."

"Good morning, sir. Auto Start and Manual Control for take-off. Pre-flight sequence initiated. All systems are ready for departure," the 'Raptor' replies.

"Thank you," I reply.

"Freedom Control, this is 'Raptor' on Freedom Hall Pad 6. Requesting Start Clearance and Departure Clearance for Brioche," I say.

"'Raptor', this is Freedom Control. Good morning, King William. You are cleared to start and depart from Freedom Hall Pad 6 for Brioche," the Freedom Controller replies.

"Start sequence initiated. All systems are ready for departure," the 'Raptor' answers.

I raise the 'Raptor' off the ground, about twenty metres, and I retract the landing skids, initiating hover mode. Slowly, I ease the thrust lever forward and I raise the nose of the 'Raptor' to a fifty-degree angle, and I activate the sub-light systems by voice command, ignoring the sub-light systems icon on the control pads. Quickly, the 'Raptor' climbs up through Freedom's atmosphere, accompanied by the Sanctuary escort ship.

Once clear of the Freedom Solar System, I say, "'Raptor', Auto Control for flight to Brioche."

"Auto Control is now active. Flight time to Brioche is forty-five minutes," the 'Raptor' replies.

After an uneventful flight to Brioche, the 'Raptor' says, "King William, we have arrived at Brioche. Do you wish to land under Auto Control or switch to Manual Control for landing?" asks the 'Raptor'.

"Continue on Auto Control please, 'Raptor'," as we approach the Earth sized world.

Brioche is like Earth, but seventy-five percent of the planet's surface is land, and the landmass is covered by a sub-tropical forest. The rest of the surface is water, and only a small percentage of land is developed, and that is where 'The Tower' is.

"Landing co-ordinates have been received," the 'Raptor' announces.

"Thanks 'Raptor'. Initiate landing at the provided co-ordinates," I answer. Eight minutes later, the 'Raptor' is on the ground, facing 'The Tower'.

A couple of minutes after landing, the 'Raptor' says, "Sir. The Sisss on board the Sanctuary ship has advised me that 'The Tower' will be speaking to you directly, via an audio com channel. The atmosphere is like the Earth's, and you can breathe it unaided. However, 'The Tower' suggests that you will be more comfortable, where you are now."

"Can you please pass on my thanks," I say.

In reply, a deep and melodious voice speaks to me, "King William 4th. Thank you for coming, I am Link One, 'The Tower' that you can see in front of your ship." Through the viewport, I can see what looks like a radio tower on Earth, only a few hundred metres away from the 'Raptor'. Link One is surrounded by trees, only a few metres high. I thought that the height of the trees reminded me of a Christmas tree farm on Earth.

"Why did you choose to speak to me directly, Link One?" I ask with curiosity.

"Normally we do not speak directly, as you may be aware, but as you are the first monarch, and first human to visit us, 'The Tower' Collective has decided that it is more respectful to speak to you directly, and we have considered the damage caused by our Sanctuary Delegate, Seetar, who has told you many lies. Also, we are aware that you are the custodian and bearer of the Golden Sceptre, which is known to us, and we understand that its objective, since it was created, was to find you and eventually merge with you," Link One explains, with deepening reverence in its voice, and Link One adds, "The Collective is happy to answer any questions that you may have."

I ask if there was any truth, in what Seetar told me. Link One networks with the other members of 'The Tower' and Link One tells me that 'The Tower' has never objected to any terraforming project in the universe before, and there is no objection to Project Genesis at all. Link One tells me that Seetar has committed several serious crimes against the Collective, and that 'The Tower' is interested in the recent audience that I had with Seetar.

I offer to share audio and video recordings of the audience with 'The Tower'. 'The Tower' accepts my offer, and I send the required files. Link One asks me to wait for it to network with 'The Tower' collective, to find a solution.

After only thirty seconds, Link One advises me that Seetar is an agent of the Karshids.

"What will you do?" I ask.

"We are arranging Seetar's detention now, and his punishment," Link One assures me, and I thank 'The Tower' for their assistance, and I officially express the desire of the White Commonwealth to establish diplomatic relations with 'The Tower' Collective. 'The Tower' agrees to this, and it says that 'The Tower' and the White Commonwealth have taken the first steps already, and they thank me for coming. 'The Tower' wishes me well, and that Project Genesis is a success. It is at this point, I realise that 'The Tower' regards me as an equal, because of the Golden Sceptre; however, I am puzzled when 'The Tower' says that the Golden Sceptre will 'merge' with me.

After the strangest meeting that I have ever had, I return to Freedom after spending only a couple of hours on Brioche. During the flight back to Freedom, I receive a message that Seetar has been detained by Sanctuary Security, at the same time as I was meeting with 'The Tower'. I touch down at Freedom Hall, much happier than before, and finally, I feel relieved that the problem has been dealt with.

Chapter Nine:

'Return to Freedom'

It was mid-afternoon when I touched down after my flight from Brioche. I ask an attendant in the VIP Apartments wing of Freedom Hall, where my sister and Charles are. The Cilex Attendant replies, "They are currently relaxing in the VIP Lounge. They have been playing minigolf, and Queen Kathryn has had a lunchtime meeting with government officials. Prince Charles was in the VIP Lounge Library, looking at Queen Noor's collection of science fiction 4D vidscreen movies."

The human colleague of the Cilex adds, "Queen Noor will be joining you for dinner, this evening. Do you want me to notify your sister of your return, King William?" she asks.

"No thank you. I want to surprise my sister. Also, can you please advise Queen Noor that I have returned, and that I will be in the VIP Lounge," I state.

"Certainly, King William," the Cilex says.

When I enter the VIP Lounge, I order a coffee from a passing servbot, and I can see Kathryn and Charles reading. The vibe between them, appeared to be relaxed, and I sensed no tension between my sister and her husband. Kathryn sees me first, when she looks up from her book, and she smiles. Charles notices Kathryn looking at me, and he jumps to his feet. The colour drains from his face, and I realised that Charles was expecting a confrontation. I pretend not to notice the look on his face, as he prepares to greet me.

"Please join us for a drink, King William," Charles says.

I look at Kathryn momentarily, and I reply, "I will join you. Thanks Charles," noting the guilty look on his face, and the respectful manner that he used. I look again at my sister, who nods encouragingly.

Hugging my sister, I quietly ask her, "How has Charles been?"

Kathryn looks at Charles, who is watching us, and she replies, "He has been fine. Charles is disgusted with himself, and the way he treated you, and Noor too."

I release Kathryn from my hug, and then Kathryn and I turn to face Charles. I point at him, saying in a deadly serious tone of voice, "Charles, your suspension has been lifted. Make sure that you apologise to Noor when she arrives. I repeat, never do this again, Crown Prince. If Noor does not accept your apology, your suspension will be reinstated, and your case will be brought before the Council of Crowns. Do you understand me, Charles?"

"Yes, Your Highness. It will never happen again," Charles replies earnestly.

"It had better not, Charles," I say, staring at Charles. The coffee that I ordered from a servbot, as I entered the VIP Lounge, finally arrives.

Before I have a chance to sit down and drink my coffee, Noor arrives and she sits down with me on a sofa, facing Kathryn and Charles.

Chapter Ten:

'Dinner with Queen Noor'

The four of us enjoy our coffee, and we talk casually for a few minutes before Kathryn asks, "How did it go, Will?" and the others look at me expectantly.

"Before I start, Charles, you have something to say to Queen Noor," I say, staring at Charles.

"Queen Noor, I would like to apologise for the distress that I have caused you, and for my breach of etiquette and trust. I made you feel uncomfortable, and I have disgraced myself. I apologise for my behaviour, and King William, I am sorry that I have brought disgrace onto myself," Charles says, looking at Noor.

I could sense Noor tensing up, on the sofa next to me, but she says quietly, "I accept your apology, Charles. Just treat me with respect, that's all I ask."

"Yes, Queen Noor," Charles says, staring at the floor.

Glaring at Charles, I say, "I accept your apology, and if there is a repeat of this sort of behaviour, you will be dismissed from duty."

"Yes, King William," Charles replies.

Finally, I say, "That's good, Charles." The mood in the room starts to lighten.

I tell Noor, Kathryn, and Charles, all about what happened on Brioche. Leaving no stone unturned, I speak for about twenty minutes, and once I finish, I let out a huge sigh of relief.

"Any questions?" I ask.

Noor looks at Kathryn and Charles, and she turns her head to face me, asking, "Did 'The Tower' suspect Seetar's involvement with the Karshids?"

I reply thoughtfully, "Not at first, but like many criminals, he started to make mistakes and he was becoming cocky. Hgh of the Helios was suspicious of Seetar's motives, and she alerted me. After speaking to the Shentar leadership, it was decided that Seetar was to be watched closely, but in a way that did not alert him."

"Cousin William, you mentioned that Seetar was associated with the Dark Emperor. My question is, did Queen Michelle as Chameleon, know about the connection between the Dark Empire and Seetar?" Charles asks. I glare angrily at Charles at first, but I start to think about what Charles was asking. To satisfy my curiosity, I pick up the handset of the IGAL commlink next to me and I call Michelle. I ask her about the link between Seetar and the Dark Emperor, and she confirms what we all started to suspect.

Michelle adds, "The Dark Emperor tried to break contact with Seetar, as she started to become quite concerned that the Karshids were going to double cross her, and that Seetar was going to seize the mysterious Kiir freighter that was destroyed three years ago."

Kathryn has a thoughtful look on her face, and she nods slowly, as Kathryn remembers a discussion that I had with Kathryn and Michelle, several weeks ago. My theory is that Seetar was the true power behind the Dark Emperor. Drago was just a passenger, but he also wanted the Kiir freighter too. I return

Kathryn's nod and I change the subject. I thank Michelle for her insight, and then I tell her that I miss her.

"I miss you too, we also need to get some healthy exercise when you get back," Michelle says seductively, and aware that the others could hear her. The grins on the faces of Noor, Kathryn and Charles needed no further explanation. Michelle laughs and she asks me, when I am coming home.

I say, "Tomorrow, my love," and we disconnect the com call.

An attendant comes over to us, and waits politely, before Noor asks the attendant, "Is dinner ready, Scarlett?"

"Yes, Your Highness. Dinner is served."

"Thank you, Scarlett," Noor replies, as we stand as one, and we move over to the dining table in the VIP Lounge.

During the meal, the mood is relaxed, and the food was perfect. We talk casually, and we share many laughs. However, I am generally silent and only join in discussions occasionally. Charles tried talking to me a couple of times, but I ignored him. Kathryn noticed my silence too.

"Will, are you okay?" Kathryn asks with concern, while Charles and Noor talk casually, as if their recent problems had never happened.

I look at Kathryn, and I reply sadly, "I miss Michelle and Caroline." Kathryn looks at me sympathetically, and she nods silently. I say to everyone at the table, "You will have to excuse me for a few minutes, as there is something that I need to check." Noor, Kathryn and Charles look at me, and Noor nods in reply. I get up and I leave the VIP Lounge, to return to the apartment that I am using.

Once I am in my Freedom Hall apartment, I pack my minimal luggage, and I say to a VIP Apartments Attendant, "Can you please let the landing pad staff know that the 'Raptor' will be departing tomorrow morning at nine a.m.?"

"Yes, King William," she says, touching her screenpad. I immediately go back to the VIP Lounge, and I note that I have been gone for about ten minutes, according to the VIP Lounge clock.

As I walk back to the dining table, I could see that the others were absorbed in conversation. Kathryn sees me first, as I approach the dining table. Kathryn nods, and the others face me, as I sit down at the table. For a moment, I just stare at the table, and then I look up, and I can see concerned looks on every face. I call an attendant over and I ask for an English Breakfast Tea. My tea arrives and I take a sip, and I place the cup on a saucer.

I look at Kathryn, who returns my stare. Kathryn recognises the signs of something that is troubling me. Turning my head, I see the same look on Noor's face too.

"Noor, I am sorry that I am not good company this evening. The strain of the problems that Seetar has caused, was starting to overwhelm me," I say, looking into Noor's eyes.

"Any time you need help, please ask me," Noor says gently. I put my head in my hands, resting my elbows on the table. Kathryn stands silently and moves around the table to stand next to me, and she puts her hand on my shoulder, saying nothing.

Charles says, "Learning from our problems, makes us stronger." Looking at Charles, I nod my thanks.

Finally, I say to Kathryn and Charles that we are leaving tomorrow at nine a.m. Freedom Time, and that we will arrive at the White Palace zone, southeast of Melbourne, Australia at one p.m. local time. Kathryn and Charles look at each other, and Kathryn says, "That sounds okay, Will."

We adjourn to the lounge area for a quiet drink. The others noticed that my mood has changed back to normal, and Noor smiled at me, pleased to see that I was relaxing.

Chapter Eleven:

'Return to Earth'

Kathryn, Charles and I depart Freedom and the Andromeda Galaxy on time and we relax in the crew lounge, with the 'Raptor' on course, travelling at low IGAL speed.

"Transit time, two hours at current speed," the 'Raptor' announces.

"Thanks 'Raptor'," I say. I focus on my companions, and I ask them about what plans they have, after our arrival.

"Studying for the flight skills assessment, a round of minigolf, have afternoon tea, and getting ready for the fly-off," Kathryn says.

"How about you, Will?" she asks.

"I need to catch up on a regal amount of paperwork, and spend some quality time, relaxing with Michelle and Caroline," I say with a sigh.

"Sounds like fun," Kathryn says, nodding in understanding.

When we arrive home, I return to my White Palace Apartment, and I open the door to my sitting room, and I enter. I hear the shrill cry of "Daddy" and I see my daughter running over to me, and I look at Michelle, who is trying not to laugh. I bend down and I kiss my daughter on the forehead, and I ask her if she has been good. Caroline turns her head and looks at Michelle.

"Caroline has been particularly good. You have learnt many new things, haven't you?" Michelle asks.

"Yes, Mummy," Caroline says with excitement.

"That's good, darling," I say, looking at Caroline.

Holding Caroline's hand, I walk over to Michelle, who gives Caroline a hug. I give Michelle a kiss and a hug before I sit down in my favourite recliner chair. Caroline's nanny, Elvira, enters the sitting room. Seeing me, she says, "Good afternoon, Your Majesty."

"Good afternoon, Elvira. How is your mother?" I ask, with concern. Elvira's father was my Science Officer on board the 'Australis' and he was my scientific adviser more recently. He died twelve months ago, and her mother was devastated.

"She is much better now. Thanks again for everything that you have done for my family, King William. It is truly kind of you, Your Majesty," Elvira sniffs, trying not to cry.

"You are welcome, Elvira. I am pleased to be able to help you. It was difficult when I lost my father, King Douglas, but every day is a new day, and I asked for help too," I say with mixed emotions.

Elvira's face brightens, and she nods silently to me, before she looks at Caroline, and asks, "Are you ready for lunch, then our visit to the Museum? Tomorrow we are playing minigolf?"

Caroline nods excitedly, and she says, "Yes, Elvira." Caroline comes over to me, and I sit forward on the recliner, so she can give me a hug and a kiss.

Caroline holds Elvira's hand, and I say, with a smile, "Thanks, Elvira."

Elvira replies, with a smile, "You're welcome," and Caroline and Elvira walk towards the sitting room door, a guard opens the door for them, and they pass through the doorway into the corridor, and out of sight.

Once Caroline and Elvira have left the room, Michelle and I

stand at the same time, and we embrace, and we walk together over to the sofa, and sit down. Before we sit right back on the sofa, Michelle and I put our arms around each other's shoulders.

Michelle and I sit in silence for a few minutes, savouring the moment together.

"Time for a late lunch. Something light," I suggest, and Michelle nods. It was at this moment, that my stomach rumbled, and Michelle laughs.

To avoid further embarrassment, I say, "Let's go."

"Okay," Michelle replies, and we stand and walk from the apartment to the Informal Dining Room. Both of us selected sandwiches from the autochef, and we take our sandwiches to a table and sit down, ordering coffee from a passing servbot.

We eat our sandwiches, as we talk casually and regularly have a sip of coffee. Once we finished our sandwiches, I talk about my trip to Andromeda. I tell Michelle everything, because I need her perspective on the events in Andromeda.

Michelle is a good listener, and she contributes some interesting points for me to consider. After talking for about half an hour, we both decide to have a quiet afternoon. Thankfully, there was nothing urgent in either of our schedules. As it was such a nice day outside, we decide to go for a walk in the White Palace Zone grounds, dressed casually. It was only a quarter to three in the afternoon. The day was warm, not hot. I was dressed in a grey t-shirt, blue track pants and grey crocs on my feet. Michelle was wearing a white peasant style, off the shoulder blouse, denim skirt and black flats on her feet.

Michelle and I acknowledge people as we walk, followed at a discrete distance by our Royal Guard escort. Michelle and I continue our discussion.

"When is the briefing for Project Genesis?" Michelle asks

me as we walk.

"Not until after the next Council of Crowns meeting, which is in a couple of days, to allow for Ann and Albert to arrive on Earth. Rebecca is already here, and Elizabeth is on her way from the White Palace Zone in the UK. King's Edward, George and James are already here. Kathryn and Charles have only just got here from Centauri," I explain.

I add, "The White Palace Zone in the US at Camp David, is now consolidated with here, and the UK."

Michelle appears surprised, and then she asks, "What is Camp David used for now, Will?"

"It is now a backup for the other two zones. Primarily, it is used for training, and it can be re-activated within forty-eight hours," I answer, knowing that it is just one small part of the plan when the White Commonwealth was established.

"Fair enough," Michelle says in reply.

Chapter Twelve:

'Family meeting and Minigolf'

Over the next two days, Ann, Albert and Edward arrive on Earth, for a couple of days break before the official launch of Project Genesis. King James and King Edward had a few days break also, for their part to play in the terraforming project, as part of the scientific research panel. I had to remind them to relax too, as I knew that they both have had several engagements recently, in several key solar systems in the galaxy. Both had arrived one week ago, after three busy weeks. Elizabeth and Rebecca have been busy as usual, and I was happy to see them, despite their hectic schedules with the White Palace Medical Service and the Sanctuary Medical Service. Therefore, our social calendar was full, and quiet times had to be planned, as the project launch was so close.

In my case, I was preparing for my first morning breakfast vidscreen appearance, and I admit to being nervous. Only Michelle knew about the upcoming appearance, and when I casually suggested to Kathryn that a hypothetical interview may take place, her response was laughter, which meant that no one had any idea about this, except Michelle. What a joke to play on the family, but the non-family members of the Council of Crowns knew about the interview, and they agreed not to say anything.

Planning for the fly-off had already started at the same time, when I had mentioned the flight skills assessment. Various members of the family were asked to select aircraft or spacecraft and fly a simulation. The choice could be from any era, or location in the universe. For the final event of the fly-off, Kathryn, Charles and I had chosen to fly the British Aerospace / Sud Aviation Concorde. I encouraged everyone to learn a new skill, and to have fun too. The fly-off helps the participants to demonstrate their adaptability, and the fly-off takes place in the Flight Simulator Centre at the White Palace, and the Galactic Navy extensively uses the Simulator Centre.

All the family and members of the Council of Crowns continued to take care of matters affecting their own solar systems, and the galaxy. Everyone was relieved that they could still catch up at mealtimes, and at social events in the evening.

Because of the size of the entourage, members of the Council and the family, had to have at least one meal in a room that I have never liked, the Royal Apartments Formal Dining Room. The family used the room for lunch, and the younger members of the family, sat at a smaller table in the room. Regularly, I sat listening to the others talk. Some members of the family noticed my silence, and they drew me into their conversations, which I did not mind. I kept looking across the table at Michelle, who asked to sit next to Kathryn. Every now and then, I noticed that Kathryn kept looking at me strangely. It was at this moment, that I realised that Kathryn had found out about my appearance on 'Good Morning, Milky Way'. Kathryn knew perfectly well that I did not have a scheduled audience with Admiral M.

During a brief lull in the conversations, I stand, and I ask for everyone's attention. The twenty members of the family, sitting at the long dining table, fall silent and they turn to face me.

"Sorry to interrupt; I have been thinking that while we have the cooperation of 'The Tower' on Project Genesis, I do need to stress that we need to be careful, because this is the first terraforming project that the White Commonwealth is managing, and we need to stay on track. The eyes of the universe are watching us." Once I finish speaking, I sit back down, and I watch the others, exchanging glances.

Kathryn looks at me, and says, "We understand, Your Highness."

"No more shop talk," I declare, and the response is laughter.

At my suggestion, Michelle, Kathryn, Charles, Rebecca, Ann and Albert go and play a couple of minigolf games. Other members of the family, who are not playing, along with several non-family members of the Council of Crowns, come along and watch the excitement unfold.

After the minigolf, Rebecca, Ann and I go to the Informal Dining Room, and we sit down in the lounge area. We talk about the relationship between 'The Tower' and Sanctuary. Kathryn and Charles chose to stay at the minigolf course, and Michelle was spending time with our daughter, before dinner. Kathryn and Charles arrive in the lounge area, not long after we arrive, and they join us.

Continuing as if Kathryn and Charles had not joined us, I say, "Somehow, the fact that I am the permanent custodian of the Golden Sceptre is the key as to why Seetar objected to the project going ahead."

Kathryn gives me a strange look, and says to me, "I thought you said, quote, 'No more shop talk', unquote." Kathryn grins mischievously, subtlety making her point, as she looks at me.

Chapter Thirteen:

'Good Morning, Milky Way'

Straight after breakfast, the Council of Crowns meet to discuss Project Genesis, as well as other major projects, and we finish at two p.m., after working through lunch. For the next twenty-four hours, there were no major events before the launch of Project Genesis, and only some individuals had minor issues to deal with.

Meanwhile, I was preparing for my first appearance on 'Good Morning, Milky Way' at eight a.m. tomorrow morning. Michelle and I spend quality time with our daughter, Caroline. We also had the chance to play some minigolf too, as a family. Later, the three of us go for a walk in the grounds of the White Palace Zone. Caroline ran around, and at the same time, took interest in her surroundings. Michelle and I sit down on a park bench together, dressed for the warm weather. Michelle turns to me, and asks, "Looking forward to tomorrow morning, Will?"

I shrug my shoulders, replying nonchalantly, "Yes, my dear." I move closer to Michelle, and I put an arm around Michelle's shoulder.

Michelle grins, saying, "You are not going to say that you are a better minigolfer than Kathryn, are you?"

"Maybe I will, but I don't think that she would be very happy with me," I say mysteriously, and we both laugh.

Michelle and I sit in silence, watching Caroline.

"Who do you think Caroline takes after, you or me?" I ask.

For a moment, Michelle says nothing and without taking her eyes off Caroline, she replies, "Both of us, I think."

For a moment, I say nothing in reply, and then I answer, "Caroline has the qualities that will make her a great Queen and Presiding Monarch. Her personality is a mix of you, Kathryn, and me. When she gets older, her resilience and drive, will give her focus. Caroline will be a trailblazer too, like her father."

Michelle says to me, as Caroline starts walking over to us, "Absolutely," and she puts an arm around my shoulder, and gives me a kiss on the cheek.

After dinner, the family relaxes in the lounge area of the Informal Dining Room. We watch video from the 'Swordfish' mission, three years ago. Michelle and I are questioned in detail about this mission, in the hours before we encountered the 'Wanderer'. I realised that this was the first time since Kathryn and Charles's wedding, when all the family has been together.

As we have coffee, Prince Albert asks me, "Sir, other than the audience with Admiral M tomorrow morning, what are your plans before the Project Genesis launch tomorrow night?"

"Not much, Albert. I do need to catch up on my regal amount of paperwork," I answer, trying not to look obvious that I was trying to avoid this question when it arose. I look at the clock on the Lounge Area wall, over the bar: eight thirty p.m. I look around at everyone, and I stand, saying, "I have an early start in the morning, please continue to enjoy yourselves," and I gesture that it is okay for them to stay seated. I say, as if it had just occurred to me, "Enjoy watching 'Good Morning, Milky Way' in the morning, I hear that they have a special guest." Before I turn around, to leave the Lounge Area, I look at Kathryn, and I knew that she knew what is going on; I nod silently in surrender as I leave the Informal Dining Room.

My alarm chimes, waking me up at a quarter to five in the morning. I go and refresh myself, and I dress smart casually. As I walk to the bedroom door, so I can exit the apartment via the sitting room, I hear a sleepy voice saying, "Good luck, sweetheart." I face the bed, and I see Michelle standing next to the bed, wearing a dark blue satin chemise. She was yawning. I go over to her, and I kiss her as I embrace her. Michelle pulls me into the embrace, kissing me, and she looks at my face. She knew that I would like to do something more intimate, but she says, "You will be late, cheeky boy," and she yawns again.

I give her a passionate kiss, and I say, "Beautiful girl."

After a silent ride in a surface transporter, I arrive at the 4D Vidscreen broadcast studios at the White Palace Convention Centre. This was the first time that 'Good Morning, Milky Way' was being broadcast from the White Palace Zone itself. Normally, the 4D vidscreen breakfast show was broadcast from the 4D vidscreen studios in Central Melbourne, at MW4HD. Quietly and quickly, I am escorted by members of the Royal Guard and a member of the vidscreen station's staff, to the studio being used. A makeup person checks my face, and lightly powders it. After makeup, I am guided into the studio itself, and onto the set in the studio. I hear gasps of recognition, as I take my seat and I look at the two hosts.

The two hosts of the program, Sarah Hitchener and Allan Koch, chat to me casually. It still amused me to some degree, the way some people fawned over me. From my own point of view, I was just an ordinary guy that happens to be King, and Head of State for trillions of beings in the galaxy.

The studio lights dimmed, and the stage lights come on. The floor manager of the studio crew starts counting backwards from ten. At zero, the floor manager points at Sarah, who starts to speak.

"It is six a.m. Galactic Time. Good morning, and welcome to 'Good Morning, Milky Way'," Sarah says to the robocamera, with a red light on top.

"We have a very special guest, this morning," Allan Koch says, to another robocamera, when its red light came on. Allan turns his attention to me, saying, "Good morning, Your Royal Highness, King William Gavin 4th, Head of State of the White Commonwealth, and Presiding Monarch of the Council of Crowns."

I reply, "Thank you, Sarah and Allan. I am pleased to be here."

"King William, what can you tell us about your recent historic meeting with 'The Tower', and how did it go?" Allan asks.

"As you know, I went to the planet of Brioche, in the Andromeda Galaxy to speak directly with 'The Tower', and I spoke to Link One, 'The Tower' that is in Andromeda, and it is the closest member of 'The Tower' Collective to the Milky Way," I answer.

"You said, directly," Sarah says.

"That's correct, Sarah. Link One told me that 'The Tower' thought that it would be more respectful for them to speak to me directly, and not through the Sisss intermediary. I believe that possessing the Golden Sceptre is a key factor. 'The Tower' was genuinely concerned with the damage caused by Delegate Seetar, who had been burning the candle at both ends, by serving the Dark Empire and his official Sanctuary Delegation. From evidence provided to Sanctuary and to me personally, it appears that Seetar had wanted to destroy 'The Tower' and then destroy enemies of the Dark Emperor, and in particular, the Galactic

Navy and me, personally," I say, to stunned silence in the studio.

Momentarily, the two hosts stare at each other, and they look at me. Before they can say anything, I say, "There is not much more that I can say on this subject, as Sanctuary Security has detained Delegate Seetar, on behalf of 'The Tower' Collective, and Delegate Seetar is awaiting transfer to the custody of 'The Tower' and his punishment. 'The Tower' wants to ensure this sort of activity does not happen again, and they regret the harm caused to the White Commonwealth. Link One desires a full diplomatic relationship with the Milky Way Galaxy."

Sarah Hitchener and Allan Koch exchange another glance, not expecting what I had just said. We go to a break, and Sarah says to me, off camera, "It is a very unusual situation," and before I can reply, Sarah is cued back in with a ten second countdown.

On camera, Sarah asks me, "King William, I understand that members of the Council of Crowns and members of the Royal Family, are currently on Earth right now."

"That is right, Sarah. Firstly, they are here in relation to their areas of expertise, for the launch of Project Genesis tonight. Secondly, all members of the Council and the members of the family, are required to maintain their flying skills, in addition to their regular employment," I explain.

Allan asks, "I have heard about the family fly-off. What is it?"

I reply, "The fly-off helps me and the senior military leaders, to ensure that each member of the Royal Family is fully prepared for any eventuality. This is a family competition, and it reflects the high standards that I expect in the Galactic Military, and develops the skills in every member of the Royal Family, because we do not know what is around the corner, for our Galaxy and home."

The two hosts nod in understanding to me. "How is your minigolf game going?" Sarah asks me, with a smile.

"Ask my wife, or my sister, for an honest opinion," I say, trying not to laugh.

The rest of my appearance on 'Good Morning, Milky Way' goes smoothly, and soon enough, my appearance on the program is over, and I return to the Royal Apartments.

Chapter Fourteen:

'Before the Launch'

On my return to the Royal Apartments, I go straight to the Informal Dining Room, and I get a ham and cheese sandwich, and a coffee from the autochef. I could sense the mood of the family members, sitting in the lounge area, watching me closely. Turning away from the autochef, I started to walk across the Informal Dining Room, and I could see grins on the faces of the family members. They were seated on the closest 'C' shaped arrangement of sofas, watching me like a hawk. I was approaching the last row of tables in the dining area, and I see a table that was free, and I thought to myself, 'Damn it, I may as well, get it over with,' and I continued walking, pretending not to notice the attention.

I sit down next to Michelle and I continue to pretend that I did not notice the scrutiny. I started to eat the sandwich, and I have a sip of coffee. Kathryn was watching me closely, as I drank my coffee, and I sneak a look at Michelle. She knew that I was looking at her because she started to smile. Finishing the sandwich, I pick up the coffee cup to drink some more coffee, and Kathryn asks, a little too innocently, "How did your audience go, Will?"

"We missed you at breakfast, my love," Michelle adds, as she puts an arm around my shoulder.

I look at my sister's face, and I glance at Charles, Michelle,

Rebecca, Ann, Elizabeth and Albert. I think quickly, but carefully, 'the best form of defence is attack', so I say, "Sorry I missed breakfast; who was on 'Good Morning, Milky Way' this morning?" while trying to keep a straight face. We then hear over the Lounge Area speakers, a music track from the 1980s, 'Video killed the Radio Star' by The Buggles. I started to laugh, and then I say to the group, "Okay, you have got me."

I stare at Kathryn, remembering the last time that I played a practical joke on her, and that was on the Copian Mission, and this was to remind me that Kathryn had not forgotten this either. Kathryn smiles at me, and she gives me a wink. I give my sister a wink in return, which she acknowledges with a smile.

It was at this moment, Kings James, George and Edward arrive in the Lounge Area.

"Great work, my boy," King James says casually. For a horrible moment, I thought that my appearance on the vidscreen program, was a disaster.

Kathryn must have been reading my mind when she says, "You were fine, King William. You did very well." Slowly, I look at the others, and they were nodding.

Michelle asks with concern, "Did we startle you, Will?" and she gives me a kiss.

In reply, I say, "No. Was there anything that we need to discuss, because the rest of the day is free until four p.m. The time of the launch of Project Genesis is at seven thirty p.m. For those that are attending, please do not be late. Thank you for your support." As there was nothing further to discuss, everyone moves onto the next activity for the day. Michelle, Kathryn, Charles and I leave the Informal Dining Room together, and we chat as we return to our apartments.

Once Michelle and I enter our apartment, we sit down on the

sofa in the sitting room. We both have an arm around each other's shoulders. For a while, we just sit silently, enjoying the moment. Michelle turns her head, and she looks at me with her soulful brown eyes, saying, "You know that if you want a career change, you could always be a vidscreen program host," and she kisses my cheek.

"Thanks for the suggestion, my love," I reply, looking at Michelle's reflection in a nearby mirror. Michelle notices that I am looking at the mirror, causing her to blush with embarrassment.

She wags a finger at me, saying, "That's naughty, cheeky boy," and Michelle smiles.

Changing the subject, I ask Michelle, "Where is Caroline?"

I turn and face my wife, as Michelle checks her screenpad.

"Our daughter is currently playing minigolf, after a visit to the Melbourne Zoo. Caroline will be joining us for dinner, as we are having dinner at five thirty p.m. This allows us to get ready for the launch of Project Genesis," Michelle explains.

"Our daughter will need an assistant soon," I say, causing Michelle to laugh.

"As we have nothing to do for a couple of hours, we could have a siesta," I suggest, causing Michelle to look at me closely.

She comes to a decision, going by the look on her face, when she smiles, saying, "That's a great idea, my love."

Chapter Fifteen:

'The Launch of Project Genesis'

After our siesta, Michelle and I enjoy an early dinner with our daughter. Caroline talks with excitement, right through the meal, and Michelle and I glance at each other, smiling as we listen to her. Elvira, her nanny, arrives to take Caroline and prepare her for bed. Michelle and I give our daughter a hug, as Elvira says to Caroline, "Caroline, you have a big day tomorrow. You have a school excursion to the Planetarium. It's time for bed."

"Okay," Caroline says, as she holds Elvira's outstretched hand.

Michelle says to Caroline, before Elvira and Caroline turn to leave, "Be good, Darling."

"Yes, Mummy," Caroline replies, as Elvira glances at me.

I give a slight nod, and I say, "You can tell me all about the Planetarium, tomorrow night."

"Yes, Your Highness," Caroline says, as Elvira and Caroline start to walk towards the door of the Informal Dining Room. As I watch Elvira and Caroline leave the room, I hear stifled laughter. I turn to investigate where the laughter is coming from, but I knew anyway. It was Michelle.

Michelle and I return to our apartment to prepare for the evening. Once we are refreshed and dressed, smart casually, I look at Michelle, and I ask, "Are you ready to go?"

"Yes," Michelle replies, with a passable impersonation of

our daughter.

I laugh in reply, saying, "Have you considered doing impersonations or stand-up comedy, my love?" I stare at Michelle expectantly.

Michelle smiles at me, as she picks up her screenpad and datapad. I pick up my screenpad and datapad from the dressing table, and Michelle says in a mock serious tone, "Time to go," and I laugh, and we leave the apartment together.

On our arrival at the White Palace Convention Centre, Michelle and I go to the conference room set aside for the Council of Crowns, to use as a breakout room. The large auditorium for the launch is the room next to us. I chat to members of the Royal Family, and the non-family members of the Council, to gauge the mood. There was nervous tension in the room, when we were advised that the assembled media contingent was ready for us. Members of the Royal Family, and the rest of the Council leave the room, and enter the auditorium, leaving Michelle and I alone. A member of the Royal Guard advises us that everything is ready for us, and we too, leave the room and enter the auditorium.

The host of the launch introduces the members of the Council of Crowns, and members of the Royal Family present, and their project responsibilities. They were all seated on one side of a long table, facing the press.

I say to Michelle quietly, as we sit down, "The Function Room where we had our wedding reception, is on the other side of this auditorium."

Michelle notices the signs that I am nervous, and she says quietly, "You will be fine."

I turn my head once I sit down, and I reply, "Thanks, beautiful girl." I see the ghost of a grin, on her face.

"Maybe later," Michelle says in a quiet, seductive voice.

The host calls me up to the podium, and as I stand, Michelle whispers, "Good luck." I give her a discreet wink, before I walk to the podium, and I place my screenpad and my datapad on the lectern.

I connect both devices to the viewscreens in the auditorium, and to the viewscreen monitor facing me. I lift my head up, and I speak into the lectern microphone.

"Good evening assembled gentlebeings of the Galactic Media, and representatives of Sanctuary Media. Tonight, is a historic occasion for the White Commonwealth. Project Genesis is the official name for the project to terraform Mars and transform it into a planet suitable for organic life," I say.

I look at the assembled media, and I glance at members of the Council, and the Royal Family. Members of the Council, and the family, nod their encouragement, and I resume speaking.

"There is a lot we know about the fourth planet, in the Earth Solar System, thanks to our own research, and with assistance from Sanctuary. We have access to more information than ever before. Three and a half billion years ago, Mars had a dense atmosphere like the Earth, and with the same composition. A large comet nucleus, with a diameter of two hundred and fifty kilometres, collided with a much larger natural satellite in orbit around Mars, which Mars does not have any more. What we have now in orbit around Mars, is a result of the cataclysmic collision. Based on datapad modelling by Sanctuary, and with assistance from astrophysicists from across the Milky Way, and Andromeda, I can tell you that the destroyed satellite, was the same size as the planet closest to our Sun, Mercury."

I pause for a moment, looking at the faces of people in the room, and I look at Michelle and Kathryn. They both nod their encouragement, and I continue, "The comet nucleus impacted the unknown Martian satellite at one hundred thousand kilometres per second, which caused the natural satellite to split into three fragments. Two fragments remain in orbit around Mars today, Phobos and Deimos. The third piece exploded outwards in the direction of Jupiter. The debris field that was the third piece, avoided hitting anything, as it travelled through the asteroid belt, and continued onwards, on an intercept course for Jupiter. However, the debris field was travelling at a velocity that would prevent it from colliding with Jupiter, and instead, it was assisted by Jupiter's gravity to gain velocity by eighty thousand kilometres per second to one hundred and eighty thousand kilometres per second. This gravity assisted speed increase gained from Jupiter's gravity, placed the debris field on a direct collision course with a small moon that orbited close to Saturn, right where the innermost ring of Saturn is now. Saturn's rings are the result of the debris field from the destroyed Martian satellite, impacting the innermost moon of Saturn, and destroying it. The conclusion of the studies undertaken on Saturn's rings, and of Phobos and Deimos, is that the destroyed Martian moon had an atmosphere as dense as the Earth, and had liquid water on the surface," as I look around the auditorium again, and I take the opportunity to have a sip of water.

The auditorium was completely silent. Michelle and Kathryn exchange glances with Rebecca, Ann, Elizabeth, Albert and Charles. Kings James, George and Edward all stare at me, stunned. Slowly and silently, everyone refocuses their attention on me again.

Taking care to be clear, I resume speaking. "The effects of the collision so close to the surface of Mars, created a gravimetric field that disrupted Mars's gravity by slowing down the rotation of Mars to what it is now. This caused violent eruptions from Mars's volcanoes, as the mantle inside spewed out, which turned Mars into a Catherine Wheel. What remained of the Martian core, rapidly cooled, resulting in the destruction of the magnetic field that Mars had. Mars lost over ninety-five percent of its atmosphere and liquid water, in a geologically short time, which was only a few days. This was a direct result of the initial collision with the unknown Martian moon. Mars and its companion satellite went from being Earth-like to what we have now, in a geologically short timescale. Thankfully, using both Sanctuary and Andromedean technology, we can now begin the most important stage of the terraforming project, and indirectly enable us to protect the Earth as well. If you look to the viewscreens in the auditorium, or at the viewscreens in front of you, I will play you a vid of the simulation of what happened to Mars. Once the vid has finished playing, the Council of Crowns will answer your questions," I say, as I touch an icon on my screenpad. The auditorium's lights start to fade, and I pick up my screenpad and datapad from the lectern. Once I sit down in my seat, I touch the playback icon on my screenpad, and the vid simulation starts to play.

After the vid simulation finishes playing, the auditorium lights fade back on to the same level as before. The host of the launch returns to the podium and steps up to the lectern.

"Before King William returns to the podium, to describe in detail the terraforming process that is being used for Mars and present a short demonstration vid, that details the process of terraforming, I would like to ask the members of the press, do they have any questions so far?" the host asks.

For about half a minute, I could see the assembled members of the press, look at each other in silence, trying to work out who was going to speak first. I look at Michelle and Kathryn briefly, and they appeared to be as perplexed as me, due to the silence. Just as the host of the launch turns to look at me, for the okay to proceed, I hear, "King William, Sarah Hitchener from MW4HD, can you please tell us, could Mars experience the same fate again, or another population centre in the solar system, experience the same problem?"

Looking straight at Sarah Hitchener, and speaking into the microphone in front of me, I reply, "Thank you for your question, Sarah. As you know, in the past, this solar system was just like any other solar system early in its formation, and it was an extremely dangerous place. Between the Sun itself and the orbit of Mars, up to forty Earth moon sized celestial bodies, orbited the Sun. This is not counting, the thousands of other objects in the solar system at the time. Collisions were common, and over time, the forty objects became the inner planets, Mercury, Venus, Earth and Mars. One of these objects became Earth's moon. The other objects not absorbed in the process of planetary formation, gradually moved into the huge gap between the orbits of Mars and Jupiter. The debris became the Asteroid Belt."

I sip some water, and then I continue, "The outer solar system had over one hundred objects that eventually became the gas giant planets of Jupiter, Saturn, Uranus and Neptune. The minor planet, Pluto was captured from the Kuiper Belt by Jupiter's and Neptune's gravity. The Kuiper Belt was formed from the remnants of the solar systems formation, and so was the Oort Cloud. Sarah, I know that this is a long-winded explanation, but I do understand that Sanctuary and Andromedean technologies, will prevent any interplanetary body from impacting any planet or population centre in this solar system. Many other solar systems in the universe use this technology."

I look at Sarah Hitchener, and she has a stunned look on her face.

"Thank you, Your Majesty. No more questions," she replies.

The host of the launch announces, "We will reconvene for the second part of the launch in thirty minutes time." The Council of Crowns, and members of the Royal Family present, leave the auditorium at the same time as the press, and take an opportunity to relax.

After refreshing myself, I return to the conference room that we are using as a breakout room. King James comes up to me and says, "Very interesting, King William."

"Thank you, King James," I reply, and I see Kathryn, Michelle and Rebecca walking over to me.

"That was really good, Will," Kathryn says, patting my shoulder in support.

"My love, that was really good. Your knowledge is amazing," Michelle says, with a smile and she kisses me on the cheek.

Rebecca says, "Well done, cousin," and she gives me a kiss on the cheek too.

"You were incredible," Charles says, as he joins us.

I nod at Charles and Rebecca adds, "I thought that you were sensational. Just like Michelle said, 'Your knowledge is amazing', and you never cease to surprise me," and hugs me.

Michelle gives me a hug too, and says, "I can't wait for the next part of the launch."

Grinning, I say, "The best is yet to come."

It was at this moment, when we are told that the members of the press, have returned to the auditorium. All of us return to the auditorium as well.

Once we are seated, the launch host glances at me, and I nod that it is okay to proceed. The launch host says to the press, "The second part of this presentation is about to start. Have all gentlebeings of the press, received their Project Genesis information packs that contain data-chips, which have vid and audio recordings, and two vid simulations, the first we saw in the first session. The second simulation shows the process that we are using to terraform Mars. King William will now present the second part of his launch address." The launch host looks around the auditorium, and then turns to me, nodding.

I walk to the podium, and I place my screenpad and datapad, on the lectern, and I start to speak. "Technically, there are three steps that we are taking to terraform Mars. These three steps have three individual stages, that need to be carried out. In a nutshell, there are nine individual stages. Information on the steps taken are in the information packs, that you have all received. We need to be aware that before we can establish a dense, oxygen rich atmosphere to Mars, the first stage is an important one. Re-starting the Martian core and mantle, reintroducing materials lost after the collision, so that we can establish a magnetic field that will protect the restored Martian atmosphere, from the solar wind, and cosmic radiation. If we do not take this crucial step, Mars would lose its restored atmosphere within ten years, and we would be back to where we started."

I pause momentarily, to drink some water, and I look at the faces of the press, watching me with interest.

I resume speaking. "Restarting the currently solid core and mantle of Mars, as well as reintroducing the materials lost, will take two to three months. Once the preparatory work is complete, then the restart of the core can take place. Experts from Sanctuary, Andromeda and Helios are working to restart the Martian core in at least two weeks' time. Without this crucial step, it would take around one hundred thousand years to terraform Mars. In the case of Project Genesis, Mars will have a stable atmosphere, protected by a stable magnetic field in about one hundred years' time. If we wanted to, the process could take just ten years, but the stability could not be guaranteed. There are several worlds in the universe with similar conditions to Mars, and since they have been terraformed to suit the organic life that are resident there, these worlds are still stable after five hundred million years. These worlds are still closely monitored, and it is rare to take corrective action. I will now play the terraforming vid simulation. Thank you for your attention," I say, as I touch the playback icon on the datapad.

The lights fade again, and playback starts.

After the vid simulation finishes playing, the lights fade back on, and there were only a few questions asked during the thirty minute, Q & A session. After the Q & A session, the launch is over, and we leave the auditorium.

I see the time on a nearby wall as we leave the convention centre: it was nine p.m.

Chapter Sixteen:

'The Collapse'

At ten a.m. the next morning, I depart for Sanctuary to deliver my report on Project Genesis, to the Delegate's Council. Michelle and Caroline join me on the twenty-eight hour flight to Sanctuary, to keep me company and to give Caroline a taste of her future role, as Queen of the White Commonwealth and Milky Way Galaxy, and as Presiding Monarch of the Council of Crowns. Caroline has already met beings of vastly different species before, and she was looking forward to meeting alien children from across the universe.

While I was occupied elsewhere, Michelle and Caroline attended an event for children of the Delegates at Sanctuary, in the Delegate's Council Precinct. Caroline was able to play with children of many different species, and they accepted Caroline unconditionally. Caroline made quite a few friends, and she was looking forward to some of her new friends travelling to the Milky Way and to the Earth. After staying at the VIP Hotel at the Shentar Transfer Station, Michelle, Caroline and I return home to Earth.

About halfway into the flight home, Caroline had gone to sleep in Michelle's quarters, and Michelle and I were in the Crew Lounge of the 'Quest'. Michelle noticed that I appeared more tired than usual.

"Will, are you feeling alright?" Michelle asks gently.

I reply, "Just a little bit more tired than usual. I did not get much sleep lately, due to the launch of Project Genesis and delivering the report to the Delegate's Council at Sanctuary. I will try to rest when we get home, and I will see my doctor when we get home," I say, not trying to dismiss Michelle's concern, as I look at her face. I move closer to her on the sofa that we are sitting on. I put my arm around Michelle's shoulders, and I put my head on the headrest and I drift off to sleep.

I wake up a couple of hours later, and I see Michelle at the autochef. Michelle must have heard me stir, because she turns around and asks me, "Would you like one?" indicating her mug of tea.

"Yes please, my love," I reply, and as I yawn, Michelle prepares a mug of tea for me. She walks over and hands me my mug, and then Michelle sits down, and she has a sip of tea. We sit in silence as we drink our tea, gazing out the viewport at intergalactic space.

Once we have finished our tea, we place our mugs on the coffee table, and Michelle asks me, "Are you feeling any better?"

"Yes, thanks," I reply, feeling better.

Michelle has a look of concern on her face again, when she says thoughtfully, "You do look better, but could you please take things easy, for Caroline and me." I knew what she was thinking, and I nod in understanding. Before I have a chance to put my arm around her shoulders, Michelle gives me a kiss, and says softly, "Thank you."

Michelle makes a perfect landing in the White Palace Hangar, and Michelle, Caroline and I return to our apartment. We have a light lunch, and we decide to have a nap for a couple of hours. Caroline is looked after by her nanny, so our rest was uninterrupted. When we wake at three p.m., both of us decide to play a game of minigolf. Naturally, Michelle beats me by two shots, and we return to our apartment to prepare for dinner.

Over the next two days, I started to notice what Michelle had already detected. I was becoming anxious, and not sleeping, but I could not identify the cause. To almost everyone else, I appeared to be my normal self, but I could tell that Kathryn knew what was going on. Michelle told me what happened next, forty-eight hours after our return from Sanctuary.

All the family was in the Lounge Area of the Informal Dining Room, and Kathryn asks me gently, if I was feeling alright. I said that I was tired, but I will be alright after another game of minigolf so that we can all unwind a bit from what has been a busy time, for all of us. Kathryn tells me, that it is a good idea, but it appeared to Kathryn that I needed some rest.

Michelle told me that I stood up without a word, and I leave the Informal Dining Room, without acknowledging anyone. Michelle, Kathryn and Rebecca, then leave the Informal Dining Room, knowing that I tended to return to the apartment or go to my private office, when I was distracted. Attendants in the Royal Apartments Complex, tell them that I went to the apartment.

Michelle, Kathryn and Rebecca enter the apartment, and they find me sprawled on my back, on top of the bed. After checking my vital signs, Rebecca contacts the White Palace Medical Service, and I wake up in hospital, two days later.

I owe my wife, my sister, and cousin a great deal.

They saved my life.

Chapter Seventeen:

'Hospital'

When I wake up two days later, I knew that I was in the White Palace Hospital. A nurse was checking my vital signs, as I woke up. I looked at the nurse, and even without my glasses, I could tell that the nurse is my cousin, Ann.

"How do you feel, King William?" she asks, as she hands me my glasses, anticipating that I wanted them.

"Thanks, Ann," I say, as I put on my glasses, and I answer her question, "I feel quite good actually," and just before Ann can reply, my doctor arrives.

"King William, as you may be aware, you collapsed unconscious in your apartment two days ago. We have conducted several tests, including tests suggested by Sanctuary Medical, and we have found the cause of your collapse, and your recent tiredness and lethargy," the doctor says.

"Which is?" I ask.

"It is a result of cellular damage, caused by the phase beam weapon that was fired at you, three years ago," the doctor explains.

"The assassination attempt at my Delegate's Residence on Shentar Two?" I ask, already suspecting the answer.

"That is correct, Your Highness. I am happy to say that your treatment is now complete, and that you will make a complete recovery, as you have responded well to the treatment. Your own doctor will check you out, when you return home, and your flight status will be cleared by her, in a few days' time. For now, you are going to be kept here for observation, for the next few days," the doctor says. The doctor leaves my cubicle, nodding to Ann waiting at the foot of the bed.

"That's good news, King William," Ann says, with a smile as she steps forward to check an intravenous drip.

"Thanks, Ann. The doctor that was just here, wasn't she the same Dr Leesa Ashdown that was on the 'Australis' working under Medical Officer Crawford?" I ask, and before Ann has a chance to reply, Kathryn, Michelle and Charles arrive.

Michelle says to me, with a look of concern, on her face, "You look much better today. The doctor has already spoken to us, and she has assured us that you will recover completely, over the next few days."

"That's right, my love," I reply, looking into Michelle's eyes.

"The Council of Crowns has cleared your schedule, for the next few days. So, take the opportunity to relax and refresh yourself," Kathryn says, touching my right arm, and taking care not to dislodge the oxygen saturation sensor on my index finger. The blood pressure cuff starts to pump up automatically, and then it deflates, at this moment, cutting off my reply to Kathryn. Michelle touches my left shoulder softly, and she gives me a kiss.

Michelle says, "I can see that you are tied up at the moment," indicating the drip in my left arm, and the oxygen sensor on the right index finger. I stare at my wife, and Michelle says, "Bad joke, sorry about that." I grin in reply to Michelle's joke. Michelle laughs, and she smiles at me, and we start to talk casually for the next thirty minutes.

My vital signs were checked several times by Ann. Rebecca arrives to take a blood sample, watched closely by the others. As

Rebecca finishes, she gives me a discreet wink, which I returned as the others talked. Not long before my visitors leave, Kathryn says to me, "When you are discharged from hospital, we have all agreed to make sure you take it easy. You do not have to worry about anything, and I understand that you will be having counselling sessions with Princess Susan, Noor's younger sister, as part of your recovery." Michelle and Kathryn give me a kiss, and Charles puts a hand on my shoulder.

"Thanks for coming," I say.

Michelle looks at the others, and says, "You're welcome," before they leave my cubicle.

Chapter Eighteen:

'Recovery and the Fly-Off'

After two days of observation, I am discharged from the White Palace Hospital, with orders to rest for a couple of weeks. Once the two week rest period is completed, my own doctor will assess my rest period, and then clear me to full flight status. My own doctor will check me every couple of days, to ensure that I am ready to resume my official role, and I was assured that no further treatment was required.

Kathryn and Charles took on some of my duties, and the Council of Crowns did the rest. For the first time since I became King, I had nothing to do, except rest and relax. No alarms to notify me of an appointment, and my diary pad was clear for the next two weeks. I could sleep in, play as much minigolf as possible, read a book, or watch a vidscreen movie. The best thing about this, was that I was able to spend more time with Michelle and Caroline.

Ann, Elizabeth, Rebecca, Albert and Kings James, George and Edward, were able to visit me in our apartment, or in the lounge area of the Informal Dining Room. We even had a couple of family barbeques, outside in the fine spring weather.

Members of the Council that were not family members, also visited me, to make sure that I was relaxing, and to pass on their best wishes. The Council of Crowns was pleased with the progress that I was making, in my recovery, and they tell me that they look forward to me returning to my role as Presiding Monarch. However, to be perfectly honest, I did not miss the stress of my role as Head of State, and at the same time, what happened to me, is a blessing in disguise, so I had time to work out ways to fulfil my role and manage my stress at the same time.

I started my counselling sessions with Queen Noor's younger sister, Susan, the day that I was discharged from the hospital. Susan is a qualified trauma psychologist, and I was fortunate that she was in the Milky Way. Like her sister, Susan is gentle, and she helped me through this difficult time, and I was grateful that Kathryn asked Noor if Susan could help. Noor was worried, and she asked Susan to see me. I first met Susan when I was at school with Noor on Earth. Susan was just nine years old then, and now she is in her early forties. I could easily compare Susan with Rebecca, as well as Noor, because they have remarkably similar qualities.

After another week, my personal doctor was able to clear me to full flight status, and she presents my clearance to the Council of Crowns. The doctor had also told me that I could return to my official duties, so long as I take regular breaks. I assure the doctor that I understand, and I set the date for my return to duty, in a couple of days, after the fly-off.

The first thing I did, was go straight to the Flight Simulator Centre, to fly a variety of aircraft and spacecraft. Michelle and I take the opportunity to brush up on flight skills and have some fun too. Besides, I had my personal honour to protect, in the fly-off.

During my recovery, I had the chance to work on my minigolf skills. The day before the fly-off, Michelle and I join Kathryn and Charles, in a thirty-six-hole game of minigolf. Much to Kathryn's annoyance, Michelle and I win easily, and Charles made the mistake of laughing at Kathryn. If looks could kill, Kathryn glares at Charles, much to my personal amusement. I offer to take a dive, and lose the next game, because I did not want my sister to be unhappy. Kathryn faces me, and we stare at each other. Kathryn started to smile, and she says, "Just play your old game, Will," and she bursts out laughing. The look on Charles's face was priceless, and he stares open mouthed at me. Kathryn, Michelle and I start laughing at the absurdity of the situation.

I change the subject, "Do not forget the fly-off tomorrow and do not be late. Study hard, and be ready for anything," I say in a casual manner.

Michelle, Kathryn and Charles look at each other, and they reply in unison, "Yes, Your Highness."

After breakfast the next morning, Kathryn and Charles, Michelle and I, as well as Rebecca, Ann, Elizabeth and Albert, meet Kings James and George at the Flight Simulator Centre of the White Palace Flight Training School. King Edward was unable to attend as he had travelled to the Shell Galaxy, on White Commonwealth business. My daughter would be watching the proceedings from the observation gallery, with Elvira. Caroline had been asking Michelle and I for several days if she could attend. Michelle and I thought that it was a good idea, as it was a good way of introducing Caroline to flight skills, before she starts flight training when she turns sixteen years old. Fortunately, Caroline loves flying, and I have already seen her fly remarkably simple simulations, with complete ease. She may be only three years old, but she already had the intellect and maturity of someone much older.

At midday, the first round of the fly-off started. Michelle and I had chosen to fly a Boeing 787 Dreamliner, from the 21st

Century. Kathryn and Charles chose to fly an Airbus A330 from the 21st Century too. Members of the family who were not flying in the fly-off itself, were in the observation gallery having demonstrated their skills beforehand. After the first-round finishes, our audience had the chance to vote, based on pilot skill, adaptability and knowledge.

Round Two starts after a thirty-minute break; Michelle and I choose to fly the NASA Space Shuttle, Atlantis and Kathryn and Charles chose to fly Apollo 11, that Neil Armstrong and Edwin 'Buzz' Aldrin flew in the first lunar landing mission of NASA in 1969. I had flown the simulation of Apollo 11 many times, and I was the instructor on the spacecraft, and I found Kathryn and Charles perfectly capable.

As a purely fun event, Kathryn, Charles and I fly the British Aerospace / Sud Aviation Concorde, which was the first supersonic passenger airliner. Michelle had joined the others in the observation gallery.

After the fly-off, which had no clear winner, several members of the family departed for their home solar systems, leaving Kathryn, Charles, Michelle, Rebecca and I together, which gave us a chance to relax for the rest of the day, as tomorrow was the day, that I formally resume my duties. We never talked shop once.

Chapter Nineteen:

'Return to Duty'

At eleven p.m., Michelle and I leave the Lounge Area of the Informal Dining Room, and we return to our apartment. Caroline had already been in bed for several hours, and after quietly checking that our daughter was asleep, we both refresh ourselves and change for bed in our respective wardrobes and bathrooms. We emerge at the same time, and we walk hand in hand to the bed, and we sit on the edge of the bed, with our arms around the other's waist.

"Thanks for taking care of me lately," I say, as I start to massage Michelle's back.

"You're welcome, my love," Michelle says seductively, as we lie down on the bed on our sides, facing each other. We kiss, and Michelle starts to massage my groin, looking deeply into my eyes.

Several hours later, we lie on our backs, with our heads turned towards each other.

Noticing that I was awake, Michelle asks, "Are you feeling any better now?"

"Yes, sweetheart. You were amazing," I reply, before I add, "We both have a busy day tomorrow. You do not need any beauty sleep, because you are beautiful already. I, however, do need beauty sleep," trying to stifle a yawn, waiting for Michelle's inevitable reply.

"Cheeky boy," she says, and gives me a kiss, while touching my groin. Michelle turns over on her other side facing the direction that I am facing. I move closer until my body touches Michelle's back. I put my arm over Michelle, in an embrace, which we remain in for the rest of the night.

After breakfast at seven a.m., I make my way to my private office, and I sit down at my desk. For a moment, I dreaded looking at my diary pad, but once I open my schedule, I was pleasantly surprised. There was nothing outstanding. I type an e-message on my deskpad, to the Council of Crowns, thanking them for their help, and their dedication to the White Commonwealth. Before I have a chance to do anything else, I receive a message from the Council, welcoming me back to my role as King of the White Commonwealth, and Presiding Monarch of the Council of Crowns.

"Thank you," I reply, out loud.

The deskpad answers, "Message sent, Your Highness."

I pick up the handset for my desk commlink, and I ask, "Assistant Bacon, has my first appointment arrived?"

"Yes sir, Queen Kathryn and Queen Michelle have arrived," Assistant Bacon replies.

"Could you please send in my wife and sister," I say in a friendly voice. The door to the outer office opens, and Kathryn and Michelle enter my office. Kathryn and Michelle stand in front of my desk. "Please sit down," I say in the regal voice, that I know annoys Kathryn, and I indicate the chairs in front of my desk, and Kathryn scowls when she sits down, facing me. "Sorry, Kathryn," I say, grinning and trying to supress a laugh. The look of mirth on Michelle's face, makes me laugh. Kathryn looks at Michelle, and she starts to laugh, realising that the joke was on her.

"How can I help you?" I ask.

Kathryn replies, "I want to welcome you back officially, to your role."

"I second what Kathryn said," Michelle says, nodding in Kathryn's direction.

I look at my wife and sister closely, and I ask, "Unofficially?" knowing that there is more.

"When is the core of Mars due to be re-started?" Kathryn asks. For a moment, I was confused. I had thought that I told my wife and sister, and then I come to understand, that I had never said much about this stage of the process yet, to either of them.

I hold my finger up, to indicate that I wanted a moment to think. Michelle and Kathryn exchange a glance, and then they nod.

I check the information on my deskpad, and I reply, "In two weeks' time," and I look at Kathryn and Michelle. "Do you want to watch a vid simulation of the core restart sequence?" I ask.

Kathryn and Michelle exchange another look, and Michelle replies, "Okay."

I pick up my screenpad off the desk and I go over to my office sofa, and I sit down. Michelle and Kathryn join me on the sofa, and we sit facing a vidscreen.

"Ready?" I ask.

Kathryn looks at Michelle, and they both reply, "Yes," and I touch an icon on my screenpad, which starts the vid simulation playback.

When the vid simulation finishes playing, I look at Kathryn and Michelle.

Kathryn asks, "Can anything go wrong with the core re-start sequence?"

I think carefully, before I answer.

"Do you recall the meeting that I had with A1 Shentar, and Raa of Helios, several weeks before the launch of Project Genesis?" I ask, looking at Kathryn, who nods, that she remembers.

Michelle says, "I remember."

"I asked both A1 Shentar, and Raa of Helios, the question that you asked. Raa said, 'Based on information on the status of Mars before the collision in the Sanctuary Archives, we already know a great deal about the conditions of the Martian core', before it solidified. Professor Lih, that you both met at the launch, is the Head Scientist for Project Genesis, and has researched this problem for some time, and assures me that the sequence used is like many other core re-starts and told me that corrective measures are rarely needed. When errors occur in the re-start sequence, they are counteracted early. Once the re-start sequence is complete, Mars will become both geologically active, and stable. The new magnetic field will continue to stabilise, and during the stabilisation of the magnetic field, work on restoring the hydrosphere and atmosphere could start," I say, looking at Kathryn to see if she understood.

"Charles tried to tell me, but I could not make any sense, of what he was saying to me. I know that it is hard to describe the process, but watching the vid simulation, has cleared things up for me," Kathryn says with a smile, patting my shoulder. I send the vid simulation to Kathryn's screenpad.

My personal commlink chimes, and I answer verbally.

"Admiral M has cancelled his appointment with you," the voice of Assistant Bacon replies.

"Thanks Aisha," I reply, looking at Kathryn and Michelle.

"As I am now free until after lunch, how about a couple of rounds of minigolf?" I ask.

"Sounds like a great idea," Kathryn says, looking at Michelle for confirmation.

The next two weeks pass quickly. At lunch, on the day before the Martian core re-start, my screenpad beeps three times. Looking at the screenpad, I say to Kathryn, Charles, Michelle, Rebecca and Susan, "All testing and simulations are complete. The re-start of the Martian core will be in twelve hours from now, twenty-four hours ahead of schedule. Midnight tonight is zero hour."

Chapter Twenty:

'Re-starting the Martian Core'

For most of the afternoon, until around four thirty p.m., Michelle and I relaxed in our apartment, and both of us, had some sleep too. Kathryn had offered to look after Caroline, so we could rest peacefully. I became concerned that Kathryn was doing too much, and I suggested that she needed a break too. Kathryn realised that I understood what she was going through, and Kathryn decided to ask Rebecca for help. Caroline adores Rebecca, and I was grateful that Rebecca was able to help Kathryn.

At four p.m., I wake up from my nap, and Michelle is still sleeping. I go to my bathroom to refresh myself, and I dress smart casually. When I emerge from my wardrobe and bathroom, I can see that Michelle is awake, as she walks over to her bathroom.

"You didn't need the beauty sleep, you are already beautiful," I say playfully.

Michelle yawns, and she smiles as she walks over to me, and Michelle gives me a hug, and says with her lips close to my ear, "Thanks, cheeky. I need to refresh too, sweetheart." Michelle kisses me on the lips, and we release each other, so she can enter her bathroom.

I sit on the edge of the bed, reading a book by Suzanne Collins, 'Ballard of Songbirds and Snakes', when Michelle comes out of her bathroom, dressed smart casually also. She looked as beautiful as always, and Michelle notices that I am looking closely at her, over the top of my book.

"Gorgeous girl," I say, and Michelle replies, with a grin.

"At least, you are not wearing black trackpants and crocs, Your Highness."

I laugh in reply, and I stand up, putting the book on a side table, and I walk over to my wife, we embrace, and I give Michelle a kiss.

Knowing that we had time to kill, before we have dinner with the family, and the Council, Michelle and I go to the Lounge Area of the Informal Dining Room. We enjoy an English Breakfast Tea, savouring every drop.

We talk casually, and we acknowledge people as they pass the sofa that we are sitting on. After a while, I fall silent, lost in thought.

Michelle asks me quietly, with concern in her voice, "Are you okay, Will?" noting that I appeared distracted.

"I was just thinking what it will be like to breathe unaided, the new Martian atmosphere," I say, after turning my head to face Michelle.

Michelle replies softly, while placing a hand on my shoulder, "I don't think that is what you are thinking, my love."

I look into Michelle's eyes, and I ask, "Do you remember after the assassination attempt on Shentar Two, three years ago, when I was thinking about abdication absolute?"

"Yes, I do. You were considering that, and not retiring," Michelle says, gently.

I nod, saying, "I realised that it is my duty, to continue as the Presiding Monarch, and that it was selfish to want to take the easy way out."

I continue, "I look at the devotion to duty of Queen Elizabeth the 2nd and her husband, Prince Phillip, in the 20th and 21st Century. For seventy years, Prince Phillip served the Queen, until his death in 2021."

Michelle looks at me closely, and replies, "I understand what you mean. You don't think that you have done enough."

"That's right," I reply, agreeing with Michelle.

"Queen Elizabeth would be proud of how you serve your planet and your galaxy. In the meantime, you need to win minigolf games," Michelle says, smiling, and she pats my shoulder in reassurance.

I kiss Michelle, saying, "Thanks, my love."

After a relaxing dinner, Michelle and I catch up on the latest news from the Net, and the vidscreen media. We return to our apartment to refresh and prepare to leave for the Project Genesis Control Room. On our arrival at the White Palace Convention Centre, Michelle and I are guided to the Project Genesis Control Room by members of the Royal Guard. Members of the Royal Family, and the Council of Crowns, who are involved in the project, take up their positions.

It was now nine p.m., and we could see live video feeds from Mars, and simulations of the core re-start, playing on the main viewscreen in the control room. At ten thirty p.m., the final preparations were made on Earth and on Mars. At eleven forty-five p.m., everyone in the control room stops talking, and the only sounds are from audio com chatter, and the live audio feeds. The atmosphere in the control room was tense, with nervous anticipation. At 11.59 p.m., every being in the room, faces me, as I sit with my finger hovering over the 'Re-start Core Sequence' icon, on my screenpad. At exactly midnight, I say, as I touch the 'Re-start Core Sequence' icon on my screenpad, "Initiate Core Re-start Sequence."

The exact dimensions of the Martian Core are well known. Devices placed in key sections of the inner core, start to melt the inner core in sequence and several nuclear detonators start to fire to start the rotation of the core. These stages are regularly repeated, as the mantle and the outer core start to rotate, and then, the rotation of the core and mantle stabilise. Over the next hour, the magnetic field is re-established, and then, it starts to stabilise.

Once we were certain that Mars had a stable magnetic field, everyone in the control room knew that the next stage of the terraforming could begin.

Chapter Twenty-One:

'Mars. A new beginning'

Two weeks after the successful re-start of the Martian core, and of the magnetic field of Mars, members of the Royal Family and the Council of Crowns not resident on Earth, start to return to their home solar systems. After a couple of days, Kathryn, Charles and Queen Noor's sister, Susan, remained. Rebecca was staying too, her rotation to the White Palace Medical Service in the UK, is now complete. Rebecca was pleased that she did not need to return to the White Palace Zone in Wiltshire, looking forward to the next stage of her career.

One day, we were having breakfast together, and I knew that I only had two audiences scheduled in the late afternoon. I was looking forward to a quiet day, and Michelle was too. After breakfast, we adjourn to the Lounge Area for coffee, before we go our separate ways for the day.

As I have a sip of coffee, my personal commlink chimes.

I take it out of my pocket, and I say with annoyance, "What is it?"

Kathryn, Charles, Michelle, Rebecca and Susan watch me closely.

Assistant Mansfield replies nervously, "I am sorry to disturb you, Your Majesty. Professor Lih, of Project Genesis is on the com for you."

With less irritation in my voice, I reply, "Okay. You can put the Professor through," and the next voice I hear, has a Helios accent.

"King William, I am happy to inform you that the core of Mars, is rotating normally, and the magnetic field is now stable. Data is now being compared with what we have in Sanctuary Archives, of Mars before the collision."

This stimulated my curiosity, and I ask, "Anything else, Professor?"

"Based on my own research, the magnetic field will be the equivalent of three and a half billion years ago. It may become stronger, as Mars continues to stabilise, but even if it gets stronger, it will not be as strong as the Earth's. The field will be strong enough to protect the atmosphere once it is restored, from the solar wind," Professor Lih explains.

"Thank you, Professor. I will see you soon," I say.

"No problem," Professor Lih replies.

I see the faces watching me, and I remember my rudeness to my assistant.

I call Assistant Mansfield immediately, "Phoebe, I wish to apologise for my rudeness before. You do not deserve to be spoken to like that."

"Thank you, sir. I know that you do not like to be interrupted, when you are with your family, and I do not like disturbing you. At least, you were not playing minigolf," Assistant Mansfield says, responding to my sincere tone.

I laugh, saying, "No problem, Phoebe."

Slowly, I look at Kathryn, Charles, Michelle, Rebecca and Susan, and I see the looks of barely contained mirth on their faces. The staff know that I am a no-nonsense person, when I am working, and after hours and socially, I am always kind and considerate.

Changing the subject, Charles asks me, "When does the next stage of Project Genesis start?"

I think for a moment, and I reply, "It is such a nice day outside, we can go for a walk in the grounds, and I can describe the next step when we take a break." The others nod, and we all go outside.

As we walk in the grounds of the White Palace Zone, we talk casually and after walking for about ten minutes, we approach a picnic table, with six individual seats that I have sat at many times before, when the weather is good. I walk ahead of the group, and I sit down.

Moments later, Michelle and Rebecca, sit next to me. Opposite me, Susan sits down, and Kathryn and Charles sit down, next to Susan. I exchange a look with Susan, who discreetly nods, knowing that I am going to discuss something particularly important, that only the two of us know about, from our time as Delegates to Sanctuary. I tell them that the re-generation of the Martian atmosphere and hydrosphere, will be starting in a few days' time.

"The Martian magnetosphere is stabilising, as the core of the planet settles down. Rotation of Mars itself, on its axis, has improved slightly, and the orbit of Mars itself around the sun, has not been affected. The gravity on Mars has increased slightly, and it will continue to stabilise too. After a century, the gravity level on Mars, will be between the Earth, and the Moon," I explain.

Kathryn asks thoughtfully, "Will, how will the gravity increase of Mars, affect spacecraft operating near Mars, and the spaceports on Mars itself?"

I look at my sister, and I reply, "As you know, today's spacecraft are adaptable, and so are the spaceports. Other planets that have been terraformed, in the way that Mars has been terraformed, have also experienced similar issues, that require reporting to the Sanctuary Terraforming Examination and Management Committee. Earth Traffic Control, Mars Traffic Control and the Earth Solar System Traffic Control, have not reported any problems so far." Kathryn nods her understanding.

While my attention is still focused on Kathryn, I notice Michelle nodding too. Michelle asks, "What information is in Sanctuary Archives about the original Martian atmosphere, and hydrosphere?" I look at Susan, knowing that this question was going to be asked.

"One million years before the collision of the comet nucleus with the original satellite of Mars, there was a scientific research mission to Mars, and the satellite," I pause for a moment, looking at the faces of the family, and Susan, watching me closely. Continuing, I say, "This mission found that both Mars and the satellite, which we have found out was called Veronya, both had dense atmospheres, and we know about the oceans and lakes on Mars. We know that Veronya had a dense atmosphere, and it had several lakes, and an ocean the size of the Indian Ocean on Earth." There was stunned silence, no questions at all.

I look at Susan again, who nods knowing that I had not arrived at the point, that I am going to make. Only Susan and I knew about what I was talking about, as we both found out the point I was about to get to, when we were Sanctuary Delegates. I must have smiled at Susan, and I could tell that everyone noticed me smiling at Susan.

"Is that all?" Kathryn asks, realising that a major point is missing. I look at my sister and my wife, and then at Charles, and finally at Susan, who was grinning.

"Are you joking, Will?" Michelle asks, becoming frustrated.

"Before I tell you the main point of our discussion, I have

mission vid and audio recordings from the Sanctuary mission to Mars and Veronya, and I will play the vid recordings on the vidscreen next to the bar, in the Lounge Area of the Informal Dining Room." I see a look pass between Kathryn and Michelle.

"I was unable to share this information at the launch of Project Genesis," I say, and both Kathryn and Michelle nod in understanding, why I was being so mysterious. I could see it in their faces.

"We also know that both Mars and Veronya, had an advanced civilisation, and both civilisations were wiped out when Veronya was destroyed. This civilisation was the equivalent of mid-21st Century on Earth," I say.

"How long have you known about this?" Michelle asks.

"Not long after I became a Delegate at Sanctuary. Susan as the Delegate for Andromeda, also knew, as we both did significant research in the Sanctuary Archives on Mars." Kathryn and Michelle stare at Susan.

"The reason why Will and I couldn't say anything before now, is to avoid culture shock. The information was never actually secret, from Sanctuary's point of view. They were concerned about culture shock," Susan explains, watching me closely.

Kathryn says to Susan and me, "Now I understand. This would have a profound effect on human history, and it could affect the history of both the Milky Way and Andromeda."

Susan and I must have looked relieved because Michelle says, "The strain of having to keep this information quiet must have been unbearable."

"That is right, my love. Susan and I discussed this issue during my counselling sessions recently. I know that we are now relieved that this is over now," I say to Michelle.

"How are you going to tell the citizens of the White Commonwealth?" Michelle asks sympathetically.

"Depends on what the Council of Crowns decide. We understand that we will have to do it. Besides, since when, have we not risen to a challenge," I say, and the others laugh, releasing the nervous tension.

I stand up, and the others follow, and we walk back to the Royal Apartments Complex, and we go straight to the Lounge Area of the Informal Dining Room.

Once everyone was settled, and facing the vidscreen, I touch the playback icon on my screenpad, for the Sanctuary Mission vid to a vastly different Mars, and the enigmatic Veronya. For thirty minutes, no one said a word, and no fidgeting either. Once the vid finishes playing, we just sit, looking at each other, and to the information that I have sent to Kathryn's, Charles's, Michelle's, Rebecca's and Susan's screen pads. No one said a word as they read the information for fifteen minutes.

Susan says, "The psychological effects of knowing this too early, could cause chaos in the Milky Way and especially on the Earth. The results would be the same in Andromeda, and on Freedom."

I say to the group at large, "It is time for lunch, and there is to be no shop talk." Everyone laughs in reply.

During lunch, I decide to go to Mars, and I want to catch up with John Hemlock, who is responsible for Project Genesis security on Mars. I am due to go to Mars soon anyway. John and his wife, Sarah, live at Opportunity Base, after moving back from the Moon. John has a daughter now, the same age as Caroline. When we finish lunch, I put my cards on the table, and I ask, who would like to come to Mars.

Rebecca has an early shift at the White Palace Medical

Service, and she tells me that she is going to Mars next week, for a five day rotation and exchange program. Kathryn, Charles and Michelle say yes. Susan expressed interest too, as she was curious about the mental health issues, that may arise from the increasing gravity and the change to the length of the Martian day.

Two hours later, Kathryn, Charles, Michelle, Caroline and Susan, were already waiting for me, when I arrived in the White Palace Hangar. We board the 'Quest' and Michelle, Caroline and Susan go to the crew lounge, while Kathryn, Charles and I take our positions on the flight-deck.

Sitting at the Command Pilot's Control Pad, I touch an icon on the control pad for internal communications.

"Prepare for Departure," I announce. Touching the icon for external coms, I announce, "White Palace Hangar, 'Quest' is now ready for departure," and I watch the hangar staff, clear the area.

"'Quest', Initiate Pre-Flight and Departure Sequence. Coms auto. Sublight and Warp Flight to Mars. IGAL systems to standby," I request, and the 'Quest' confirms my instructions.

"Manual Control for Departure, auto control for approach and landing on Mars. I may request auto control for the flight to Mars," I say, adding to my instructions. The 'Quest' confirms my additional instructions.

After a textbook departure and climb through Earth's atmosphere to space, I order, "Auto control," and the 'Quest' takes control.

"Transit time to Mars at Warp 1 is thirty minutes," the 'Quest' announces.

Thirty minutes later, we descend through the still thin, Martian atmosphere, and after passing through the atmosphere containment field, we touch down, and the rooftop hangar doors close. A boarding tube connects to the port side of the 'Quest', and after shutting down the ship, we exit through the boarding tube, and we enter the arrivals lounge of the VIP hangar. Our group is greeted by John and Sarah. The group splits up and Michelle and Caroline are shown around by Sarah, while Kathryn, Charles, Susan and I go with John, to the main control room on Mars for Project Genesis.

As we walk to the control room, I had noticed the increased gravity, and I had noticed that the atmosphere in the base seemed to be more natural. John said that they are using the equivalent atmosphere of what the new Martian atmosphere will be like. I ask John if he is enjoying his job as Head of Security for Project Genesis on Mars.

"I am enjoying it, and the hours suit the family," he replies.

"Thanks again, John, for the recovery of the Golden Sceptre. You have served the White Commonwealth with dignity and honour. I know that my father, was grateful as I was in the middle of the military operation to destroy the Dark Empire at the time, which diverted some of the Empire's attention, away from the Golden Sceptre," I say to John as we walk.

"You are welcome, King William," John replies.

We enter the Project Genesis Control Room and Professor Lih gives me an update on the status of the Martian Core. The room shakes slightly, and one of the technicians in the room says, looking at a viewscreen, "Two point five on the Richter scale, no aftershocks."

Professor Lih says to me, "That was a small Mars quake; the quake we have just felt, is a typical one."

"What would a strong Mars quake be?" I ask.

"Over six on the Richter scale," the Professor answers.

"Any reaction from Olympus Mons?" I ask, pointing in the

direction of the volcano, and highest mountain in the Solar System, one thousand five hundred kilometres to the east of Opportunity Base.

"It is smoking now, as we have restored the Martian volcanos. As the atmosphere is still thin, the gases are venting into space. The other volcanos are venting too, but within the range expected," Professor Lih explains. I turn and look at Kathryn, Charles and Susan, and they nod in understanding.

We leave the Project Genesis Control Room, and we go to the VIP quarters. Michelle, Caroline and Sarah, were in the VIP Lounge Area, and we sit down with them. Caroline was extremely excited, and I smile as I listen to my daughter. Kathryn and the others were smiling as well.

I look at Susan, and I ask, "Have you noticed anything in relation to the mental health of the beings living and working here, in a changing physical environment, as a result of the increased gravity and the higher rotational speed of Mars?"

"The length of the Martian day could be a problem in the weeks and months ahead. In relation to the gravity increase, the effects are less profound, but not less important. I understand that the White Commonwealth Medical Service, and Sanctuary is monitoring the situation closely," Susan says, looking at me.

"Thanks Susan," I say, with a nod. I look at Kathryn and Michelle, and I ask them for their insight. Both agreed that what Susan said, was important.

Charles asks, "What about the air pressure and temperatures rising, as the atmosphere becomes denser?"

I look at Charles, and I reply, "The issues would be like the gravity increase, and stabilisation of the length of the Martian day. All issues dovetail each other."

Chapter Twenty-Two:

'A sad end, to a long life'

When Kathryn, Michelle, Caroline, Susan and I, return to Earth, after six hours on Mars, I receive a coded message on my deskpad, while sitting at my desk in my private office. I run the decryption sequence, and for a moment, I am shocked. I re-read the e-message again, and I pick up the handset of the desk audio commlink.

"Assistant Mansfield, are you aware of the e-message, that I have just received from Alpha Centauri?" I ask, trying to keep the emotion out of my voice.

"Yes, King William. King Edward at Alpha Centauri received a message from Queen Noor's husband, King Edward, about King George. The Prime Minister has been informed, and she has expressed her sympathy. The news has not been announced yet, and the Council of Crowns has not been informed either," Assistant Mansfield replies, sounding like she did not want to upset me.

"Thanks, Phoebe, I will inform the Council of Crowns. Can you please contact my wife and sister, and ask them to come here, as soon as possible? If they ask why, please tell them that I will be giving them a triple alpha security message. And Phoebe, I know that you have worked for my uncle, and I thank you for your concerns, I do appreciate it," I say, my voice faltering.

"That is alright, Your Highness. Aisha is here, helping me,"

Phoebe answers.

A few minutes later, Kathryn and Michelle stand before my desk, and I motion for them to sit down. Seeing the look on my face, Kathryn and Michelle exchange a look, knowing that I have something bad to say.

I say, "A few minutes ago, I received a message from Andromeda, and Alpha Centauri that King George of Proxima Centauri, during a state visit to Andromeda, was tragically killed when his personal shuttlecraft, exploded when it tried to dock with his IGAL ship, the 'Brave'. After an extensive search, nothing remains of the 'Brave', the shuttlecraft or my uncle, King George. The White Palace Protocol Office has confirmed the message."

Both Kathryn and Michelle are speechless, but they see the look on my face, and they can see tears starting to appear. Michelle and Kathryn stand, and they come around the desk, and they sit next to me on the office chairs that they were sitting on. They both place a hand on my shoulders, as I start to cry. Michelle says sympathetically, "Will, I am so sorry to hear that. Take the rest of the day off if you need to. We can inform the Council of Crowns for you."

"I am so sorry, Will. Is there anything you need? I know that you will have to make the official announcement, so take it easy, until you need to make the announcement," Kathryn adds.

I look at Michelle and Kathryn, and I reply, "Thanks. If one of you could inform the Council and cc me the e-message, I would appreciate it."

"Yes, sir," Michelle says, looking at Kathryn for confirmation.

"Before you go, we need to remember that the White Commonwealth still needs to function, and I ask that everyone, remembers that we still have work to do. King George was in his late nineties and he was still fit and healthy, and his vitality and enthusiasm for Project Genesis was crucial. We will hold a memorial service for him, once investigations by White Commonwealth Security, and Andromedean Security are complete. I want no speculation as to the cause of the incident, or blame attributed to anyone. If you could note what I have just said and send it the White Palace Press Office, and could you please advise them that I will address the Galaxy within the next half hour. It is business as usual for Project Genesis, and everything else," I say in a decisive and normal voice.

I stand up and I walk around the desk, and I stand facing my wife and sister. "Thanks guys," I say, with the ghost of a smile on my face. Michelle gives me a hug, and she kisses me.

"Thanks, beautiful girl," I say, trying to lighten my mood.

Michelle kisses me again and she says, "I will inform the Council for you now," and she sits at my desk typing an e-message on her screenpad. I see her touch the 'Send' icon.

Kathryn gives me a hug, and she kisses me on the cheek.

"Will, are you going to be okay?" Kathryn asks with concern.

"Yes. I will be. The show must go on. Michelle, did you send the message to Sanctuary too?" I ask.

Michelle nods, saying, "Yes, I did."

"Excellent, I say. If they offer any help, please accept it," I say, thinking carefully.

"Before you go, you know about the research that King George was doing on the Dimension War?" I say, looking at Kathryn and Michelle.

Michelle looks at Kathryn, and says after seeing Kathryn nod, "You mean the research that he has been doing, almost all of his life?"

"That is correct," I say.

I point to the coffee table in the office, and on it, were a couple of desk pads, a screenpad and a small box, the size of a briefcase. I walk over to the coffee table, and Michelle and Kathryn follow me over, and we sit down on the sofa, next to the coffee table. I open the box and I show them the huge collection of data chips. Michelle's eyes widen as she sees the labels on the data chips, and when Kathryn looks at the data chips, her eyes widen too.

"I know the sequence, that we have to use to access the data chips. We can look at them in the weeks and months ahead, as we have the time, with Project Genesis under way, and we can start looking at them after the memorial for King George," I say mysteriously.

At this moment, Assistant Mansfield enters my Private Office and says, "The vid screen media crew is here for your address. They have set up in the audience room."

"Thank you, Phoebe," I say as Phoebe leaves my office, for the audience room.

Kathryn, Michelle and I stand again, and I say, "You know about the culture shock concerns with Mars and Veronya?" Michelle and Kathryn nod, looking at the open case of data chips. I close the box up, and I take everything on the coffee table, and I place the items onto my office desk, and I activate a 4D hologram.

"A stealth shield?" Michelle asks.

"Everything will be completely safe. We are going to look at these data chips soon, because the contents will change history, hence the cloaking system. Many things will be confirmed, and many questions will be raised too. The vids and audio clips, as well as documents, prove how the Dimension War started. Knowledge of the contents on the data chips will have a profound effect on universal history, and I can say that this information is the key to the future."

I leave my Private Office, accompanied by my wife and sister, when Michelle says, "You will be fine."

Kathryn adds, "Just be yourself."

Just before I enter my audience room, I see Michelle and Kathryn, walk down the corridor to their own offices. A Royal Guard member opens the audience room door, announces my arrival to the vidscreen media crew, and I enter the room for the announcement that I am going to make.

The End – *Project Genesis*
(Book Three in the Sanctuary Series)

E Mare Libertas (From the Sea, Freedom)

Other books in the Sanctuary Series:

Published by Olympia Publishers
Sanctuary (Book One) by Gavin Catt
Prelude to Sanctuary (Book Two) by Gavin Catt

Coming Soon in the Sanctuary Series:
The Dimension War (Book Four) by Gavin Catt
Sanctuary: Destiny (Book Five) by Gavin Catt